What the critics are saying about...

4 stars "The plot will keep you scrolling as fast as you can. There are many twists to the plot and some of them will definitely catch you by surprise. There are a couple of characters in this book I hope get their own stories soon. I will definitely be on the lookout for future releases by Ms. Adams." ~ *Nicole La Folle for Timeless Tales*

Four stars "Adams pens a delightful tale, with introspective characters and a magnificent conflict. The characters' emotions gently progress, while the story flows at a wonderful pace." ~ *Robin Taylor for Romantic Times Magazine*

"The sex is scorching hot and the verbal sparring is just icing on the cake. Ms. Adams has a winner with MIDNIGHT! I hope she has more sassy characters waiting in the wings." ~ *Denise Powers for Sensual Romance Reviews*

"Midnight was a seductive, whimsical read; with a dry, humorous look at vampire cult fiction and movies. Elisa Adams brings an enjoyable and sensual tale to life." ~ *Michelle Houston for Sensual Romance Reviews*

4 *Roses*"The characters were engaging, and the uniqueness of the story was greatly appreciated. My favorite parts were undoubtedly the superbly written love scenes. The steam was practically rising from the book during the intimate moments." ~ *Natasha for A Romance Review*

ELISA ADAMS

DARK PROMISES I

MIDNIGHT

An Ellora's Cave Romantica Publication

www.ellorascave.com

Dark Promises: Midnight

ISBN #1419950495

Edited by: Martha Punches
Cover art by: Syneca

Electronic book Publication: February, 2003
Trade paperback Publication: June, 2005

Warning:

The following material contains graphic sexual content meant for mature readers. Dark Promises: Midnight has been rated *E-rotic* by a minimum of three independent reviewers.

Ellora's Cave Publishing offers three levels of Romantica™ reading entertainment: S (S-ensuous), E (E-rotic), and X (X-treme).

S-*ensuous* love scenes are explicit and leave nothing to the imagination.

E-*rotic* love scenes are explicit, leave nothing to the imagination, and are high in volume per the overall word count. In addition, some E-rated titles might contain fantasy material that some readers find objectionable, such as bondage, submission, same sex encounters, forced seductions, etc. E-rated titles are the most graphic titles we carry; it is common, for instance, for an author to use words such as "fucking", "cock", "pussy", etc., within their work of literature.

X-*treme* titles differ from E-rated titles only in plot premise and storyline execution. Unlike E-rated titles, stories designated with the letter X tend to contain controversial subject matter not for the faint of heart.

Also by Elisa Adams:

Dream Stalker

Just Another Night

Demonic Obsession: Dark Promises

Shift of Fate: Dark Promises

In Moonlight

Dirty Pictures

In Darkness

Dark Promises: Midnight

Chapter One

Amara walked out of wardrobe, her thigh-high, four-inch-heeled, artificial leather boots making a horrible rustling sound with every step she took. She might as well have wrapped her legs in trash bags. It would have had the same effect.

She tugged at the top of the black vinyl bustier, trying in vain to contain her breasts. When were these people going to learn that there was a huge difference between a B cup and a D cup? *Whoever designed this costume ought to be shot.* They seemed to get skimpier and skimpier with every film.

She'd thought it was bad enough when she'd had to stuff herself into those leather pants for the first film. By the second, the pants had been changed to a mini skirt, which was later changed to a micro-mini and a halter top. It amazed her that, as the films gained popularity and the budget skyrocketed, the material used in each costume got smaller and smaller. You'd think they could at least afford something that would cover her ass.

"You doing okay, Amara?"

She turned, her hands on her hips, ready to take out her frustrations. As it just so happened, the director, Robby Baker, appeared in the hall. "No, Robby, I'm not. I can't even move in this getup. I don't understand how you expect me to run around like this. I can barely walk without some part of my body popping out."

"Come on, Amara. For your age, you have a terrific body."

Her age? She didn't realize that thirty-three had suddenly become over-the-hill.

"A lot of women have to pay to get tits like yours. They're not naturally blessed like you, honey."

The last time she considered herself "blessed" in the breast department was in eighth grade. Then she learned how much *fun* it was to walk around all day with two mounds the size of grapefruits hanging from her chest.

"I'm not going to flash my breasts for the camera. If you want that, you can find someone else."

"Well, that's kind of what we need to talk about." He pulled her into an empty room at the end of the hall, quietly shutting the door behind them. "The new producers want to take the Midnight films in a different direction."

Shit. That was never a good sign. Were they planning to kill off her character? She certainly hoped not. It was Midnight who had made the films so popular in the first place. Well, Midnight and her human nemesis-slash-lover J.T., but without Midnight the movies wouldn't have much of a plotline. "Go on."

"Okay, what they want is to give the movies more of an...adult flavor."

She snorted. "We're not exactly making kiddie flicks here. Isn't an R rating good enough for them?"

"Well, actually, no."

She stared at him for a minute, trying to figure out if he was joking. He wasn't. "Damn it Robby, I'm not going to get involved in a porn movie!"

Robby sighed and paced the room. "Listen, Amara. The Midnight franchise isn't as popular as it was when we first started. With your face and your tits, we could make a killing if we added a little more spice. Derek agreed, the rest of the regular cast agreed. It looks like you're the only hold out."

"What is this sudden obsession with my chest?" She was looking for one good reason why she shouldn't strangle him for *that* comment. She clenched her teeth and her hands, willing herself to keep calm. "I'm not going to have sex on camera, no matter how much money it will make."

"Get over yourself, babe. There's been a couple of hot sex scenes in all five of the Midnight movies. Hell, you were only twenty-four when the first one was filmed. What's a little more skin, anyway? You'll be protected, if that's what you're worried about. Derek will wear a condom, if that's what you want. You won't have to worry about catching any diseases."

Did everyone think she had no morals? "There is a huge difference between simulated sex and real penetration." She shook her head and yanked up her bustier one more time. "It's not going to happen."

"It's just Derek, honey. You know, your fiancé? Please don't tell me you two have never had sex."

"What Derek and I do in our bedroom is none of your business, and it's most certainly not going to be exploited for the sake of making money."

Robby ran a hand through his dark, greasy hair. "Funny, but Derek didn't voice a single objection."

That stopped her cold. "He didn't?"

"No. As a matter of fact, he seemed pretty excited about doing it on camera with you."

Derek was a dead man the second she got home. "I'm *not* doing it."

"You don't have much of a choice."

"Is that some kind of a threat?" She crossed her arms over her chest, but had to uncross them when the skimpy top puckered indecently. Robby didn't miss the eyeful of cleavage she'd just unwittingly treated him to. His eyes widened and his smile grew, and she would have smacked him if he wasn't holding her fragile career in the palm of his oily little hand. Instead she glared at him, and he had the decency to look humbled.

"Of course not, honey. I would never threaten you. But face it, where would you be without these movies? Have you had any other offers lately?"

No.

Playing Midnight Morris in that first movie had been the best and worst thing for her career at the same time. Sure, the first movie had branched out into four sequels and a line of merchandise that involved everything from action figures to cereal to clothing, but it also killed her hopes of ever being taken seriously in Hollywood. To the entire population of casting directors, it seemed, she *was* the bubbly blond vampire and was therefore unsuitable for any other role.

Still, she wasn't going to compromise her principles by getting horizontal with some beefcake on film, even if the beefcake in question was the man she was supposed to marry in two weeks. It didn't matter how much money the film might gross. She'd learned that money wasn't everything, especially when her dignity was involved.

Sure, she'd spent a good portion of her adult life playing a campy, comic book style vampire with more boobs than brains, but she had to draw the line somewhere.

"I'm not doing this, Robby, and that's final."

"What can I say to make you change your mind? What do you want, more money? A bigger house? A sports car?"

"How about none of the above?" She narrowed her eyes and looked down at the little man. She wasn't overly tall, but the four-inch heels combined with his small stature gave her the advantage. He backed up, but held his ground.

"Is that your final answer?"

She nodded, her lips pursed.

"Well, then I'm sorry. I'm going to have to let you go."

"I don't think so. I have a contract." They weren't going to get away with this.

"By refusing to follow the director's and the producer's orders, technically you're now in breach of contract."

"That's bullshit! Nowhere in my contract does it say I have to fuck my costar." Right after she got out of this scrap of a costume, she was going home to call her lawyer.

"But it doesn't specifically say you don't have to, either."

The nerve of that man! To think, at one time in her career, she might have considered him a friend. "You can't do that."

"No, I probably can't." He winked at her. "But I could tell the producers about the little private party you had a couple of weeks ago in the company limo."

"You wouldn't dare!"

Robby shook his head. "What would everyone think of their golden girl then? Just you and three men in a limo with God only knows what kind of drugs and alcohol." His smile widened. "I'll bet the tabloids would have a field day with that one."

She sucked in a breath, trying to find some way out of this one. Unfortunately, there didn't seem to be any. It wouldn't matter that nothing had happened in the limo. It was just her, Derek, and a couple of his old frat buddies from college. She didn't sleep with any of them at the time, and the strongest substance in the vehicle at the time had been beer.

But it was her word against everyone else's, and she'd been known to throw a wild party or two in her day. She'd been threatened that if she had any more, she'd lose her job.

What would she be without this role? Just an aging chick with a bad dye job and a liberal arts degree from a community college back in Vermont.

"What do you want me to do?"

"Just get naked for the camera, sweetheart, and Derek will take care of the rest."

She shook her head. There was no way she could go through with this. As much as she enjoyed her job, there would be others. It was a devastating blow, but she'd get over it. After a couple of months, the hubbub would die down and she'd be able to start auditioning again. Surely someone out there would want her for something.

"This is *so* not going to happen. I have to go home and talk some sense into Derek."

"Oh, I don't think you're going to change his mind."

The hairs on the back of her neck prickled. She didn't want to hear what was next, but she had to ask anyway. "Why do you say that?"

Robby laughed. "He's not as inhibited as you, I guess. Why don't you take a look at this while you're home wallowing in your self-pity."

He tossed her a VHS tape. "What's this?"

"Just Derek's latest project. Enjoy, honey. I know I sure did."

* * * * *

"Derek?" Amara walked through the door of the townhouse they shared. She was greeted by silence. *Strange*. He should have been home by now.

She shrugged and set her purse on the coffee table, glad to be rid of the vinyl bustier. Her skin would probably itch for weeks. She poured herself a glass of wine and popped the tape into the VCR, curious about what Derek had been working on behind her back. As far as she knew, the only things going on with his career were the Midnight movies and a couple of cell phone commercials.

The title "More than Friends" flashed across the screen, followed by Robby's name as director. She blinked hard when she saw Derek's name next. Just what the hell had he been doing? He'd always thought independent films were beneath him. Why was he suddenly starring in one, and doing so without telling her?

She learned a lot more than she wanted to when the film opened and a naked Derek strutted across the screen, obviously very aroused. Oh, he was really in for it when he got home.

What surprised her more, although she should have been expecting it after Robby's comments, were the four naked women following him. When one of them, a tall skinny redhead with obviously fake boobs, encircled his cock in her hand Amara had to turn the movie off.

"That son of a bitch!"

If she hadn't been so mad, she might have heard the noise sooner. But she'd been too stunned by what she'd discovered about Derek's secret to notice. She sat on the couch, remote in her hand, for a good five minutes before the squeaking bedsprings registered as something other than the anger churning in her head.

She jumped off the couch and bolted up the stairs, taking them two at a time. She threw open the bedroom door, expecting to find Derek with the redhead from the movie. Her jaw dropped when she saw he was fucking Steve, the caterer who lived next door.

"Holy shit!" She couldn't believe what she was seeing. "What the hell do you think you're doing?"

"Hey, baby." He didn't even have the decency to look contrite. Instead he continued to thrust his cock, a cock that would *never* find its way inside her body again, into Steve's ass.

Steve, on the other hand, looked totally mortified. His entire body turned bright red and he closed his eyes, but Derek wouldn't let him go.

"Why don't you get naked and join us, Amara? I've been telling Steve all about your fabulous body."

That was *so* not going to happen. "You're never going to get the chance to see me naked again, buddy."

"Oh, come on, Amara. Have a little fun for once. It wouldn't hurt to spice up our sex life a little."

"Is that why you're with Steve, and why you made those movies? To spice things up? Geez, Derek. If you were bored you should have just said something."

"Boring doesn't even begin to describe you in bed, babe. I need so much more than you can give me." Derek's eyes rolled back and he sighed in sheer pleasure. "Steve is so much better than you are. Do you know that? He'll suck my dick whenever I want, and he doesn't get sick at the thought of swallowing."

He was actually getting off on this. "You're a scumbag, Derek."

"I just want to have fun. Come on, Amara. We could all get off together."

Poor Steve had gone beyond red. He was now a lovely shade of purple. He squirmed to get away, but Derek's huge hands kept him right where he wanted him.

"Are you high again, Derek?"

That got his attention. He stopped pumping and pulled out of Steve. The man scrambled to get his clothes and ran out of the room. Amara heard the front door slam a few seconds later.

Derek's face went ashen. "How can you even ask that? You know I gave that stuff up months ago."

And apparently he'd picked up some other bad habits. She didn't know which one she hated more—the coke or the indiscriminate sexual encounters with anything moving "I think you should leave now. Pack your shit and go. *Do not come back*!"

"We'll get through this. We've been through worse, and we always make it through okay." He reached for her, but she ducked away.

Her stomach churned at the thought of his hands on her skin. "How long have you been gay?"

"I'm not gay. I like women, too."

"Oh, yes. That's right. I watched enough of that tape to know women get you hard, too. How many times have you cheated on me?"

He gave her a solemn look. "None. I love you too much."

"*None?* What the hell did I jut walk in on, a prostate exam?"

Derek sighed, looking a lot more annoyed than he had a right to. "I've never slept with another woman, Amara. Not once since we got engaged."

"What about those women in the movie?"

"They don't count. I was getting paid for that. And the men don't count, either. That's not really sex."

Was he making this up as he went along? "How many men have there been?"

She watched him count to ten on his fingers and then furrow his brow. "I'm not sure. I lost count last month sometime."

She closed her eyes and took a deep breath, willing herself not to smack him. He deserved it, but he wasn't worth breaking a nail or two over. She didn't spend hours filing and polishing for nothing. "*Get out!*"

"That's not fair. You interrupted, so you should at least give me some relief."

"Excuse me?"

"I'm still hard. Why don't you suck me and make it better?"

"You've got to be kidding me. No cock that's been poking around in someone's ass is going to be getting within two feet of any part of my body." She lifted Derek's robe off the floor and tossed it to him. "Get the fuck out of my house. I'll pack up your stuff and you can hire someone to come pick it up later."

He clicked his tongue. "Does this mean the wedding is off?"

"Oh, I don't know. Maybe you can marry Steve or the silicone-enhanced redhead instead."

Chapter Two
Two months later

Amara sat at an outdoor café, leafing through the classified ads for the second time that morning. Until an acting gig panned out, she had to find something. She'd gone on every single audition her agent had set up for her, and even a few she'd set up behind his back, and still she was jobless.

She took a sip of her coffee, not really tasting it. It was her fourth cup of the morning, and she was starting to feel the effects of the caffeine. Her hands were shaking as she tried to turn the newspaper page.

Or maybe the shaking was caused by the article she'd read in the entertainment section. It seemed Derek wasn't faring nearly as badly as she was. Not only did he get to stay on the Midnight cast, he had also recently signed on to do a major network sitcom and a string of commercials for a soda company.

She blew out a breath and crumpled the paper. Her life just sucked. Why was it that Derek, the biggest freak she'd ever met, got all the breaks when she was left all alone? He probably had sex with the producers and the film company execs, male and female. That would explain a hell of a lot in this mixed-up situation.

Not for the first time she got a prickly feeling, like someone was watching her. She looked around, but no one seemed out of the ordinary. Rather, she lived on the outskirts of Los Angeles and *everyone* seemed out of the ordinary. No one stuck out, though, at least not that she could tell. Still, she couldn't shake the strange feeling that she was being watched.

In the past couple of weeks she'd had a couple of instances where she thought she was being followed. When she turned around, no one was there. She was probably being paranoid, but she had a strange knot in the pit of her stomach. It had been building for a while, but something told her today was the day. Something was going to happen.

She wasn't going to wait around for it to happen *here.*

She was about to leave when a woman came up and tapped her on the shoulder. "Excuse me. I couldn't help but notice you look just like the woman who used to play that vampire. What was her name? Twilight? Sunset?"

Amara lifted her hand to shield her eyes from the bright light of the sun. "Midnight. That's me."

The woman shook her head. "No. That's impossible. That woman died."

"What?"

"I read it in the National Gossip yesterday. That's why she was replaced with that other girl. You know, that Mitzy Anderson. All the magazines say she's going to star in the next movie, since the original actress is gone now."

"No, I'm not dead. I *did* play Midnight Morris in the first five films."

The woman turned to her companion, a middle-aged man. "What was her name? Emily something or other?"

This could not be happening. "My name is Amara. Amara Daniels." A few months ago, she was the hottest thing in town. Now everyone thought she was dead? She was willing to bet that Derek and Robby had something to do with that bit of gossip.

"That doesn't sound quite right." The woman frowned and shook her head. "I could swear it was Emily. Emily Douglas?"

Oh, for heaven's sake. This was getting her nowhere. "How did the Gossip say she died?"

The woman shrugged. "Something about silicone poisoning. An exploding breast implant." Her eyes lit up. "Yes, that was it. Do you remember when we saw that movie, Peter? I told you then that those breasts had to be implants. I guess I was right."

Now Amara was fuming. Call her names, lie about her death all they want, but don't ever call her breasts fake. These babies were real, and she had the straining back muscles to prove it.

"I hate to disappoint you, but you're wrong." She glared at the woman. "They're real."

"Heavens, dear. I don't know what you're getting so worked up about." The woman shook her head and put her hands on her hips. "You're taking this much too personally."

That was it. She wasn't going to sit around and listen to this for another second. She gulped the rest of her coffee, left a couple of bills on the table, and stalked away from the couple. As she walked down the sidewalk she could hear them still talking about silicone-induced deaths and Mitzy Anderson. She wanted to scream.

* * * * *

Midnight Star Dies from Implant Poisoning.

Marco crumpled the trashy newspaper in his fist, tossing it into a trashcan as he walked by. Ninety-nine percent of what was reported in that paper was garbage, but every once in a while a story held a grain of truth. He'd seen her a couple of days ago—he knew she couldn't be dead, but some part of him refused to accept the story as a lie until he saw her for himself.

He paused on the sidewalk outside her townhouse. He couldn't sense any noise or movement inside. She wasn't home, but at this time of the day, that was nothing new. He thought he might know where he could find her—at the little café where she read the paper most mornings.

His fixation with her had started a few months ago, when he'd happened to catch her latest movie. Although he didn't approve of the subject matter, Amara Daniels had intrigued him from the first. She inspired in him both fascination and aggravation, which had led to his obsessive behavior of late—behavior becoming increasingly difficult to control.

What had started as an innocent curiosity mixed with a dash of anger had turned into something more, something he didn't quite understand. Something he didn't want, but there was nothing he could do about it. He'd felt like this one other time in his life, and that had ended horribly. He couldn't let that happen again, yet he couldn't seem to stay away.

The café was just a short distance from her townhouse, but the sun blaring on his back bothered him to no end. He adjusted his sunglasses and kept his head down until he could get under the shelter of one of the umbrellas that covered the tables. Once there, he sighed in relief, both to be relatively protected from the sun, and because *she* was there.

This time she wasn't alone. An older couple stood next to her table. The woman appeared to be arguing with Amara. He strained to hear what was being said, but was only able to catch the end of the conversation before Amara got up from the table and walked away.

She headed in the direction of her townhouse. His car was parked there, so he had no choice but to follow. He kept his distance, though, not wanting to spook her. Women these days were unpredictable. She was just as likely to attack him as call the police if she felt threatened.

She went inside, closing and locking the door behind her. He stayed back, but he was close enough that his ears could pick up the metallic slide of the deadbolt lock clicking into place. He should have left then and there, having proven that she was indeed alive.

He didn't.

He leaned against his car, his gaze focused on that locked door. It was nothing to take personally—she didn't even know he was there, but somehow he felt slighted. He closed his eyes and groaned. This was getting to be too much. He had to do *something*, before this obsession took over his life.

* * * * *

Amara sank down onto the couch, tears welling in her eyes. This was it. She'd auditioned for everything she could find, and nobody wanted her. She was washed up at thirty-three, and she didn't have a single marketable skill to fall back on.

She probably should have listened to her college advisor when he'd told her a liberal arts degree wasn't going to get her very far. At the time she'd blown him off, telling him she was going to be a big star someday. Acting was all she'd ever wanted to do, but her current step-father from hell had insisted she go to college for at least two years. If she'd listened to someone, anyone, who'd offered advice, she might not be in this situation now.

Her savings would cover her for a little while longer, but pretty soon she was going to have to find a job, preferably one that didn't involve serving greasy french fries or taking off her clothes. Unfortunately that seemed to be all that was available.

So *what* was she supposed to do? She'd scanned the classifieds for two weeks and had yet to come up with an opening for an ass-kicking, lipstick wielding, party loving female vampire with a love of all things dark and dangerous. The closest thing she could find was a salesgirl at a local sex shop, and somehow she doubted that would pay very well. The perks would be good, *if* she had a man, but she was going to try being single for a little while. She was still reeling from Derek's trip to the other side.

A knock at the door stopped her thoughts short. She got up to answer it, wondering who would bother to visit a dead woman. If it was the press, which was a definite possibility, she wasn't prepared to deal with them. She was still in a funk from her messed up life and couldn't be held responsible for her actions.

She reached for the doorknob, but pulled back. A feeling of trouble hit her hard, like a physical blow. She closed her eyes and took a deep breath, waiting for the feeling to pass. It usually did. This time it didn't. She should just walk away, pretend she wasn't home. She couldn't. She *needed* to open the door, even knowing that opening it would change her life forever.

She gulped and unlocked the deadbolt, the sharp click of the lock sounding hollow and grim. She'd *felt* things before, but never anything like this. She'd never sensed that she was in actual danger, but helpless to do anything about it. The knob turned easily in her hand and she swung open the door, unable to shake the sense that she was inviting her own doom.

One look at the man standing there and her mouth went dry. A cold sweat broke out on her brow and she shook her head. She'd seen him before, around the café a few times. His presence had never bothered her there, but there was a big difference between sitting a few tables away and having him standing so close she could feel the tension that radiated from him. If she'd been able to get her legs to move, she would have run away screaming.

His hair was brown, with the faintest hint of lighter brown streaked through it. It was cut fairly short, but long enough on top to look ragged. His eyes were a few shades darker than his hair, so deep they could almost be called black. There was something about him she couldn't quite pinpoint, something that had the hairs on the back of her neck standing on end.

She swallowed hard before speaking, hoping to hold onto that last little thread of composure. He probably had a very good reason for showing up on her front porch, looking like some kind of maniac. "Can I help you?"

"Are you Amara Daniels?" His voice was deep, almost hypnotic, and very faintly accented. Was it Spanish? Italian? She couldn't be sure.

"Um, yes." She spoke slowly, cautiously. She tried to figure out what it was about him that had her senses on high alert, ready to fight or flee at his slightest movement. It could have something to do with the dark expression, the dark clothes, and the dark stubble that lined his jaw.

Or it could be the fact that he was at least six-three, built like a linebacker, and had placed his foot in the open door so there was no way she could close it.

"I thought so." His eyes glittered with a strange light, almost animal-like. He regarded her with an arched brow, his expression a cross between intrigue and anger. She involuntarily backed up a step, trying to figure out a way to get the door closed so she could get to the phone to call the police.

"I won't hurt you." He gave the door a quick shove and was inside before she could do anything. He slammed the door behind him and locked the deadbolt. "Not much, anyway."

She backed into the kitchen, blindly reaching behind her for the phone. She picked it up and lifted the receiver to her ear. The line was dead. Her heart raced and a thin film of cold sweat broke out over her brow. She did not want to end her life like this.

"What do you want?"

He took the dead phone out of her hand and set it on the counter. He skimmed a finger along her jaw. "I want to teach you a lesson."

"*What?*" Her voice came out as a squeak. "I've never even met you. What did I do to you that made you want to hurt me?"

He shook his head and clicked his tongue. "Do you really think your actions in those movies don't have consequences?"

Oh, God. This guy was a total psycho. "I didn't do anything. I've never tried to hurt anyone. Those movies were just movies. I don't know what you're talking about."

"Don't you?" He smirked. "In your world, vampires are all-knowing. Of course, you have no idea what we are really like."

We? She blinked at him. Did he really think he was a vampire? "What did I do to you that has you so angry?"

He sighed deeply. "It's just you, Amara. Just you."

He continued to stroke her jaw, and she couldn't stop the little tingle that ran through her. She was scared out of her mind, but there was something else there, something harder to define.

Something she *refused* to define, since the man was obviously certifiable.

"What are you going to do to me?"

"I'm going to show you the truth." He smiled, but there wasn't a hint of gentleness in it. "You *will* understand, no matter what I have to do to get through to you."

He fisted a hand in her hair and pulled her head back. "Do I make myself clear?"

"Clear? Oh, yes. Crystal. I promise not to make fun of vampires anymore. I will be a good little girl and—"

"Shut up!"

"Sorry."

He narrowed his eyes at her, the set of his mouth grim. "*Not another word.*"

She clamped her mouth shut and swallowed hard. Her vision faded, and the last thing she saw before she hit the floor was the deadly look in his eyes.

Chapter Three

Fuck.

Now what was he supposed to do with her? It would have been much easier to walk her to his car. He couldn't exactly fling her over his shoulder and carry her out. Surely she had nosy neighbors. All of these snotty little neighborhoods did.

He looked down at her, a twinge of guilt knifing through him. He hadn't meant to scare her this badly.

Or had he?

Maybe. Impulse control wasn't exactly his strong point.

She was a lot smaller than he'd expected. On the screen she'd looked so big, like a larger-than-life fashion doll with her obviously dyed bleach-blonde, teased into a puffy mane and eighteen pounds of makeup covering her face. She had those big breasts, too, but he'd wondered if they might be real.

Lying in a heap on the kitchen floor, her light brown hair fanned out around her, she looked almost frail. But even through regular clothes, he could see a hint of that killer body he knew she possessed—the one she flaunted with abandon in the movies.

He had to stop that train of thought right now. If he was going to teach her any kind of a lesson, and he definitely planned to do just that, he would have to carry out his original plan. His plan most certainly did not involve admiring that incredibly curvy body in any fashion—as much as he'd like to. Later, there would be plenty of time for that. Now the question remained, how was he going to get her home?

"Hey, Amara. Wake up."

Nothing.

"Amara?" He bent down and shook her lightly. She stirred, but didn't open her eyes.

Wonderful. He should have planned this better. If he'd just sat down and thought about it a little longer—

Without leaving him much time to react, Amara jumped up and took a swing at him. Something hard clipped him on the side of his face. She pulled her arm back to swing again, but he was ready for her this time. He grabbed her wrist and squeezed. She cried out and dropped whatever it was she'd been holding, the object clattering to the floor.

"Let me go!"

He snorted, holding her off with minimal effort. He had to admit, though, that he hadn't expected her to be this strong. For such a little thing, he could picture her holding her own easily with almost anyone.

But not him. She wasn't any match for him. No woman was, and he made sure they were all aware of that. "Why don't we take a little ride in my car?"

She stilled and glared at him. "Is that some kind of a euphemism for sex? Is that what you want from me?"

He laughed. "I'm not looking for sex." Although seeing her in person may have changed his mind on that. "I just want to talk to you for a little while."

He rubbed his jaw, which was aching a little from her blow. "What did you hit me with, anyway?"

"A teakettle."

"A teakettle?" He'd been shot at, stabbed, run over, and stuck in more life-threatening situations than he could count, but no one had ever smacked him in the face with a *teakettle* before. It was a little unsettling that she'd tried to beat him up with a kitchen tool. What was she going to do next, try to give him a haircut with a cheese grater?

"If you come willingly, this will be much easier."

She shook her head. "That's not going to happen."

"Then I guess I'm going to have to make you very uncomfortable." He pulled a length of twine cording from his jacket pocket and bound her hands behind her back. She struggled, and it almost shamed him that he was enjoying her fear.

Almost. He couldn't quite make himself feel the remorse he should probably feel.

He shouldn't be feeling bad. In the back of his mind, somewhere, he knew what he was doing was wrong. But this fixation he'd developed had clouded his better judgment. He'd feel the guilt later, probably more than he could handle, but now he just felt the need to find a way to rid his thoughts of her.

She ground the heel of her boot into the top of his foot in a last ditch effort to save herself. He laughed at the idea of such a little woman getting the better of him. It had never happened before, not even while he was human, and he wasn't about to let it happen now. He started to tighten the bonds around her wrists even more, but changed his mind at the last minute.

Instead, he pulled her against him so her arms were flush with his chest, her hands dangerously close to his cock. He made the mistake of inhaling her scent, a rich blend of cinnamon and spice, and it nearly drove him out of his mind.

He resisted the urge to groan and reminded himself that he was here for a reason other than sex. Although the thought of getting her naked in his bed held more appeal by the minute, he had more important things to do first.

Pushing aside her hair, he leaned in and licked the tender skin of her neck. "Do you know what I'm going to do with you?"

"The only thing I want you to do is let me go." She wiggled against him, unaware that every movement sent a jolt of fire through his body. Her fingers brushed his rapidly hardening cock. He could feel how hot they were even through the fabric of his jeans. He inhaled more of her spicy scent and fantasized about what her blood would taste like.

He *would* taste her, possibly in more ways than one. But not yet. He resisted the urge to sink his fangs into her delicate flesh for a small sample. For now, he contented himself with tasting the fear that lingered on her skin, along with a sweet, almost sensual note he hadn't planned on.

"I have big plans for you, Amara. I can't wait to get you home and get a taste of the hot blood I can feel pounding in your veins."

She shivered. When she spoke, her tone was meeker, more uncertain. "If you let me go now, I promise not to press charges. I'll pretend like this whole thing never happened."

"When I'm through with you, my dear, I'll make sure it will be impossible for you to forget."

She whimpered and her legs seemed to give out. She leaned hard against him and he sucked in a sharp breath at the feel of her wrists rubbing against his cock. She had to know how hard he was, it would be impossible for her not to feel it. He shoved her away and paced the room, trying to get control of himself before he did something stupid like rip off her clothes and take her right there in her kitchen.

He grunted and slammed his hand into the wall. He would *never* allow himself to touch her intimately without consent. No matter how much he suddenly wanted to, he wouldn't take her without her permission.

At least not in the sexual sense. He'd come here with the intention of taking her back to his house—keeping her there until she'd learned her lesson—and he wasn't going to stop because of a stupid little attraction he felt towards the woman.

"Let's go." He grabbed her arm a little too roughly, trying to compensate for his uncharacteristic lack of control over his body.

"Where do you think you're taking me?" She stumbled and he had to slow his pace so she could keep up. He drew in a few deep breaths to steady his rapid breathing. When he was finally ready to face her, he was able to plaster some semblance of an evil smile across his face.

"I can't tell you until we get there. That would ruin the surprise."

He led her out to his car and had to fight with her to get her into the passenger seat. At one point she opened her mouth to scream, but he quickly clamped his hand over it.

"That wouldn't be a very wise idea."

She bit into his palm and he dropped his hand. The second he let go she yelled at the top of her lungs. "Somebody help me!"

A few people stopped to stare.

He stuffed Amara into the passenger seat and held up his hand. Holding her in place with one hand, pressing hard against her shoulder, Marco motioned to the passersby on the street. "Move along folks. I'm a bail recovery agent. This woman skipped out on a bond, and I have to bring her in to the police station."

They accepted his lie without question, going back about their business like they hadn't just seen him put a woman with her hands tied behind her back into his car.

He laughed, thinking that couldn't have happened anywhere but New York or L.A.

He buckled the seat belt around Amara and closed the door, walking around to the other side of the car and getting behind the wheel. Once he had the car on the road she turned to him.

"You're a scumbag." She shifted in the seat, adjusting her hands. "Worse than a scumbag. You're…you're…"

"Believe me, honey, I've been called so much worse than you can even imagine." He stopped at a red light and turned to her. "You'd be a lot more comfortable if you faced forward and rested your hands flat against the seat back."

"Go to hell."

"I've already been there. It wasn't so bad." The light turned green and he turned left, heading toward the highway that would take them back to his house. "Why don't you just relax and enjoy the ride? We're going to be in the car for a while."

She turned her nose up at him in a gesture that was almost comical and looked out the window. Her voice was haughty when she spoke. "If you're not going to take me back home this second, I'm not going to talk to you for the rest of the ride."

That was fine with him.

* * * * *

Oh, wasn't this just *perfect?* It had been bad when she couldn't find a job, but being unemployed was nothing compared to being spirited away to some isolated house in the middle of the woods with a lunatic that thought he was a vampire.

She rubbed her wrists, still red and sore from the rope he'd bound them with. He'd told her they wouldn't hurt so much if she'd sat still instead of trying to work her arms free, but did he really expect her to sit there and allow him to kidnap her without trying to free herself? The fact that she didn't have a master's degree did not make her an idiot.

At least he'd untied her hands when they arrived. If there was one thing she couldn't stand, it was being totally at the mercy of a man—especially when the man outweighed her by at least a hundred pounds and was probably in desperate need of his daily medication.

She looked out the window into the fading daylight. Even if she had been able to get the window up, she wouldn't have been able to do anything about it. Her room was three stories up and rocks littered the ground below. If she even survived a fall that far, she'd be too broken to get away. Until she could find a way downstairs, she was stuck.

"Are you hungry, Amara?"

She spun, startled. She hadn't even heard him come in. She expected him to be standing in the doorway, but he was less than a foot away. She backed up until her back was pressed against the cool window.

"Amara?"

She opened her mouth to speak, but couldn't seem to make a sound. She shook her head, hoping he'd just go away. Food was the last thing on her mind right now. She just wanted to be home, relaxing in a warm bubble bath with a good book and a pint of her favorite ice cream.

"You don't want anything?" His voice was low, almost seductive in tone. She blinked, not sure where *that* thought had come from. The last thing she needed to be thinking about was seduction.

Although, if it would save her life…

No. That was a bad idea, no matter how she looked at it. Even if he wasn't a total nutcase, she didn't even know his name. "I'm not really hungry. Being kidnapped by a man who threatens to suck the life out of you tends to do that to a woman."

He laughed. "Suck the life out of you? I would never do that."

"Isn't that what *vampires* do?"

"Of course not." He shook his head, his expression annoyed. "Why is it that you humans will believe anything you read in a book or see in a movie? In my opinion, real life experiences always count for so much more."

"Oh, and I suppose you're some kind of authority on the lives of *real* vampires?" She snorted, getting a little irritated herself. "Tell me this, hot shot. If you're the vampire you seem to think you are, how could you come to my house, in broad daylight, and push your way inside without an invitation?"

"Ah, the wonders of Hollywood." He took a step closer and she wished there was some way she could melt into the window and disappear. "Tell me, Miss Daniels, do you always believe everything you see on television without question?"

"No. That would be a stupid thing to do."

"Then how can you pretend you know about my kind? In truth, most of you closed-minded humans have no idea."

She rolled her eyes. In spite of her fear, this conversation was getting out of hand. "You seem to be forgetting a very important fact. Vampires are *fiction!* Everything about them is make-believe."

"You think so?" His lips curled into a humorless smile, revealing gleaming white fangs that had to be almost an inch long.

She blinked hard a few times, sure those hadn't been there a few seconds ago. Laughing shakily, she tried to make light of the situation. "Wow. We could have used your makeup artist on the last film. Those are good. They look almost real."

"Almost, huh?" He walked forward until his body was just barely brushing against hers. "What would you do if I told you they're very real?"

He ran his tongue along the fangs and she gulped in a breath. They couldn't be real. Vampires were just like every other thing termed supernatural, a byproduct of someone's vivid imagination.

"What if I told you I've seen better?" She scoffed at the fangs, but there was a little voice of doubt inside her. She stomped it to death without much effort. "You have to let me go. Someone will come looking for me sooner or later."

He shrugged. "I don't see why. You've done nothing but yell since you got here. If I were someone close to you, I'd be happy for the vacation."

"You can't talk to me that way! I've got an agent. I've got a huge townhouse and a really big car. I've got a whole line of Midnight merchandise with my picture all over it." She narrowed her eyes for effect. "I've got *action figures!*"

He laughed outright at that. "How nice for you. It must be wonderful to be immortalized in eleven and a half inch plastic."

She didn't find any of this very funny. "Say whatever you want. You're not even real. I probably bumped my head when I fell, and I'll wake up in my own home with a splitting headache."

"Trust me. I'm very real." He leaned closer until his lips brushed her neck. "And you may not be very hungry, but *I* am. I'm thinking you would make a very nice meal."

Oh, God. This man was crazier than she thought. She'd faced rabid, demented fans a time or two in her career, but she'd never been about to be turned into someone's bedtime snack.

"Wait! Don't do anything rash. Whatever it is you want from me, we can work it out."

He said nothing, but she could feel his lips curl into a smile against her throat. She gulped, wondering what it would take to get him to back off.

Or what it would take to get him closer.

She took a deep breath and willed herself to concentrate on the situation at hand. If she remained rational, she'd be able to find a way out of this without getting hurt. Probably. "Who are you, anyway?"

"Marco."

"What's your last name?" Maybe she'd recognize the name from some of those demented fan letters she got every so often.

He shook his head. "Just Marco. I don't normally use anything else."

"Okay, Just Marco. Why don't we make a deal." She struggled to keep the quiver out of her voice. He had to feel how hard her pulse was pounding.

"No deals." He pressed his hands to the window, one on either side of her head.

She sighed, a little too close to the edge of insanity herself. If she let her rational side slip one more notch, she was going to totally lose it. "Please listen to me for a second. My life has been really, *really* bad lately. I lost my job and my fiancé in the same day, I haven't been able to find a decent job in months, and now this. I'm about a second away from losing my mind, and I don't think you want to be dealing with a hysterical female right now."

"I really don't care." He brought his gaze up to meet hers, his expression indifferent. "Yell, scream, and cry—whatever you need to do. No one will hear you all the way out here. It's just the two of us."

She blew out a breath. She'd just about exhausted her options here. "Are you trying to scare me?"

He lifted a shoulder in a careless shrug. "Maybe."

She *was* scared, but she was also getting angry. She had a feeling he was toying with her, taunting her to purposely get her upset. He was taking some kind of sick pleasure in her confusion. She wished she had something around to hit him with. She didn't dare use her hand—the man looked so solid she'd probably break her knuckles.

"Tell me something," he said. "What's the fascination you humans have with vampires?"

She raised an eyebrow. "What does it matter to you?"

"Watching everything being done wrong is getting a little old. I can't believe anyone would actually want that kind of a job."

"Look, buddy, I needed that job. It doesn't really matter why I did it, just that I was good at it."

The corner of his mouth rose in a half-smile. "That's not quite the word I'd use to describe your performance."

She sucked in a harsh breath, fisting her hands at her sides before she did something irrational like attempt to break his nose. "I had to do what I was told. That was the nature of the job."

He laughed. "And I'm sure someone held you at gun point, forcing you to dress in next to nothing and run around like a brainless sexpot."

"Oh, and what would you have liked me to do, continue living in a rat-infested studio apartment, waiting tables at a trashy bar to pay the bills?" She'd done *that* for a long time before she got a break. She wasn't about to give in to some psycho with delusions. "The Midnight series was the best thing that ever happened to me."

This was just crazy. She'd heard some horror stories about stalkers before, but this beat them all hands down. It was her own fault for opening the door and inviting him to take over her life, but in the end it wouldn't have mattered. He would have found another way in. He didn't seem like the type to give up easily.

Vampires *were* fictional. If she kept repeating that, maybe she'd be able to ignore the fangs that protruded from between his lips and the hungry gleam in his eyes she doubted had anything to do with food.

"Marco?" Her voice was more of a whisper than the forceful command she'd intended.

He raised an eyebrow but said nothing.

"You don't actually drink blood, do you?"

He smiled slowly. "Do you want to find out?"

Chapter Four

She shook her head. "*No!*"

Marco did something unexpected. He burst out laughing. "You look like you're going to pass out again. Please don't do that. It was bad enough the first time."

Indignation rose in her, sharp and fast. She wasn't some sissy girl who couldn't handle herself when things got a little rough. "I did not pass out. I…I was faking it."

"Not at first, you weren't."

No, she hadn't been. But what did he expect? Getting kidnapped by an escaped mental patient with a vampire fixation wasn't exactly an everyday occurrence. "Yes, I was. And stop laughing at me."

"I'll stop laughing when you stop acting like a fool. I'm not going to hurt you. I told you that before."

"Much."

"What?" His expression was confused.

"Much," she repeated. "You said you weren't going to hurt me much."

"Did I?" He shook his head, his eyes clouding over. He looked mildly alarmed for all of five seconds before the smile was back. "I guess you'll just have to wait and see."

His smile widened and she noticed the fangs had gone away.

"How did you do that?"

"Do what?" He leaned against the footboard of the gigantic bed that took up a good portion of the room. His stance was casual, but she had a feeling he was baiting her.

"Make those fake fangs go away."

"I have control over them. They come and go as I want them to. At least, most of the time." He winked at her. "I know you're having a hard time believing this, but they're not fake."

"Oh, okay." Yeah, this made a whole lot of sense. Not only was he a vampire with razor sharp fangs, they conveniently disappeared when he didn't want them there.

"I can prove it."

She shook her head, not sure she liked the sound of that. "Just knock it off, okay?"

She turned away from him and looked out the window again. It was now completely dark outside, the inky blackness a sharp contrast to the bright lamps in the bedroom. Her eyes widened at the sight of her reflection in the glass. She looked like she'd been run over by a dump truck.

Her hair was matted in some places, snarled in others, her clothes were impossibly wrinkled, and there was more mascara running down her cheeks than there was on her eyelashes. The least Marco could do after he'd kidnapped her was give her a hairbrush and a washcloth. Self-consciously swiping a hand through her ratty hair, she turned to ask him for something to wash up with.

She screamed when she bumped into a solid wall of male chest. Stumbling back, she looked up at Marco and blinked hard. How did he get there? Just a second ago, he'd been standing halfway across the room. "How did you do that? Is this some kind of trick?"

"I can move very quickly and silently when I want to."

"But you...I...no, no, *no.*"

"As you will find out, sweetheart, some of your little human legends are fairly close to the truth."

She gulped. "Do you teleport around or something?"

"Not exactly." He leaned over her neck and drew a deep breath, shaking his head as he moved away. "It's more a matter of being in total control of myself. I can move across short distances faster than your eyes can follow."

She gaped at him, not able to form a single coherent sentence. Two things registered in her mind—one, the man was either very quick or some kind of an illusionist, or two, she might want to start rethinking her views on the existence of vampires.

Chapter Five

Marco had walked out of the room soon after the little show, giving Amara some time to let it all sink in. She needed some time to think about everything before she accepted him for what he was. He could see in her eyes that she wanted to believe him, but something was holding her back. Most likely, her Hollywood lifestyle had jaded her so much she no longer believed in anything but her next paycheck.

In a way, she wasn't the only one who was jaded. He'd lived a long time, and he'd seen a lot of things that made him angry. He'd been angry enough to kill many times, though he'd never given in to the temptation.

He'd never kidnapped anyone, either.

When had this situation gotten out of control? He really had no excuse for what he'd done. He shouldn't have taken her, but he'd gotten so agitated, so obsessed that he'd snapped. He'd had a few occasions in his life where he'd been close to blind with fury, but only one other instance came close to this. It was one he'd tried most of his life to forget, but knew he never would.

This was absolute madness. He should let her go back to her life, but for some reason he couldn't bring himself to do it. When he was close to her, he couldn't account for his actions. Her arrogance spurred his anger and curiosity even more, and her fear enticed him in a way it shouldn't.

What upset him the most was how much he wanted her. He thought getting close to her, learning that she wasn't the woman he'd thought she was, would be enough to turn him off. She *wasn't* what he'd thought, but it didn't help get her out of his head. There was something about her that drew him to her. He'd been angry with her when he'd taken her. Now he didn't know what he was.

Why had he put her in his bedroom? There were so many other rooms in the house to keep her in. Her comfort should be nowhere near the front of his mind. She didn't deserve the best suite in the house, but he couldn't very well move her now. He'd made the mistake of taking her, and now he was going to have to deal with it.

He shook his head as he walked down the hall toward one of the spare bedrooms. He'd put her in his room because of one reason. The second he saw her in person, in jeans and a tee shirt instead of artificial leather and gallons of makeup, he knew he had to have her.

But he couldn't.

After the way he'd abducted her, Amara would never agree to anything. She would also never understand the desire that coursed through his veins whenever he got within ten feet of her. She wouldn't understand that, for some reason, he fed off the fear he sensed in her as much as the desire he'd seen in her eyes.

And it had been there. She would deny it, but he'd seen it. She wanted him as much as he wanted her, and she wasn't happy about it, either.

He wanted to possess her.

Shaking his head, he tried to get rid of this temporary madness. He found women attractive, but certainly not necessary in the grand scheme of things. They were temporary playthings, enjoyed briefly before he threw them away in favor of a younger, fresher model. They were most certainly *not* something to keep.

Ever.

He couldn't keep the human woman, no matter how much his delusional mind thought it wanted to. She was not his to take, and she was *not* his to keep. She had her own life, one he knew nothing about, and she wouldn't take kindly to being made into the permanent pet of a four hundred year old vampire.

He stopped outside his locked bedroom door, knowing the only thing that separated him from the temptation on the other side was the flimsy piece of wood and the even flimsier lock. It would keep her inside effectively, yet it would never keep him out if he lost control of himself and went to her.

He pressed his palm to the door, feeling the beat of her heart through the wood. Was it his imagination, or did her blood begin to beat a little faster in her veins?

He shook his head, chalking it all up to spending entirely too much time acting like a lunatic. She was probably sound asleep, giving no thoughts to him other than those of most painful revenge.

He left before he could no longer rein in the urge to go to her and ravish her like the animal he was. Right now, sleep was in order. He would figure out what to do with Amara after he got a few hours' rest. He'd been awake for more than twenty-four hours, and it was time to recharge before he faced her again.

*****

Amara sat on the edge of the bed, absently changing the channels on the small TV she'd found inside the armoire next to the bed. She didn't have a watch and there were no clocks in the room, but she could see the light fading outside yet again. It had been an entire day, and her stomach was loudly protesting the prolonged absence of food.

She got up from the bed and pounded at the door. "Hello! I need food in here! Come on, Marco, even prisoners on death row get treated better than this."

She hit the door as hard as she could until her fists went numb, but it was no use. She got the same response she'd been getting all day.

Nothing.

Here she was, getting ready to waste away, and Marco the Vampire was probably in bed getting his beauty sleep.

She'd stayed awake most of the night thinking about it. As much as she hated to admit it, she'd been kidnapped by what appeared to be a living, breathing vampire. Or at least she *thought* he lived and breathed, but she couldn't be sure. Fictional ones didn't, but when she'd been flush against his chest he'd felt *very* alive to her. Especially the part of him that responded to her wriggling.

That part had felt impressive, even through layers of fabric.

She raised her hands to pound on the door again, but they hit nothing. The door was open, and she was pounding the air. She looked up, right into Marco's dark eyes. Eyes that looked sleepy, glazed, and more than a little bit annoyed.

"*Oh, shit.*" She backed up an involuntary step.

He pushed his way into the room and set a tray down on the bedside table. "Did I happen to mention that I'm a bear when I haven't had enough sleep?"

She winced inwardly at his growling tone. "Oh, I'm *so* sorry. Next time I'll just starve until you feel up to feeding me. I guess I'm not very well-versed in kidnap victim's etiquette."

He narrowed his eyes. "There's some food. I'm going back to bed."

A sudden panic hit her at the thought of him walking out and locking the door behind him. "Wait!"

He turned, his arms crossed over his chest. "What?"

She had no idea what she wanted to say to him, but as strange as it sounded, she didn't want to be alone. She had so many questions to ask him. Hey, if he expected her to learn more about vampires, she had to do her research, didn't she?

"Don't you need to eat?"

He gestured to the tray of food. "I don't need to eat that."

"But can you?"

He shrugged. "If I had any desire to, but after a few hundred years it all starts to taste the same."

A few hundred? *Oh, boy.* "Um, do you always sleep all day?"

He nodded. "I do when I don't have someone here trying to break down doors and crack my eardrums."

She rolled her eyes. "Deal with it. I know you can go out in the sun, since you came to my house in the middle of the afternoon. Why do you sleep during the day if the sunlight doesn't bother you?"

"It does bother me. I'm very sensitive to the sunlight, but it isn't fatal unless I stay out too long. It's much more comfortable to sleep during the day, and be awake when it's dark." He sighed and yawned. "Is there anything else you need, or can I go back to bed?"

"Look. I've been alone since last night in a strange house with nothing to do but watch fuzzy television shows on a set smaller than my laptop screen. You don't even have cable. Forgive me for wanting a little normal conversation."

And the more she found out about him, the easier it would be to figure out a way to get away from him. He was strong, she'd give him that, but no one was invincible.

"I am not capable of *normal* at six in the evening."

"Humor me." She sat down on the edge of the bed and picked up half a sandwich from the tray. She wrinkled her nose as the pungent smell of peanut butter hit her. "Yuck."

"Deal with it. It's all I have in the house."

She sighed and took a bite, swallowing it quickly so she didn't have to taste it. She set the rest of the sandwich back down on the plate. One bite was plenty for now.

Marco stood in the doorway for a long time before he sighed and came into the room. To her disappointment, he closed and locked the door behind him, pocketing the key and locking them both in the room. "Just in case you get any ideas." He flopped onto the bed and closed his eyes.

There had to be another way to get out of this. If she'd learned one thing in the endless parade of stepfathers her mother had subjected her to, it was how to take care of herself in the face of threatening men. Although Marco appeared far less threatening lying flat on his back across the bed with his eyes closed and his arms sprawled over his head.

Wondering if he was sleeping, she poked him lightly on the side. Big mistake. In one swift move he had her pinned to the mattress, his big body covering hers.

"Don't ever do that!"

She whimpered at the feel of him over her. "Um, sorry."

He shook his head. "You still don't know what you're dealing with, lady."

She licked her lips—a nervous habit, but apparently Marco took it to mean something else entirely. His eyes darkened impossibly and he crushed his mouth over hers.

He forced his tongue between her parted lips and she thought she was going to pass out right then. A kiss, especially with a man she didn't even know, wasn't supposed to be *this* good. She should push him away, tell him where to shove his presumptuous ideas.

Instead, she embarrassed herself by moaning into his mouth and wrapping her arms around his neck. She hadn't felt like this in a long time—maybe never, and she was damned well going to let herself enjoy it. She could worry later about the fact that he was a total nutcase who had kidnapped her.

Marco pushed a hand under her shirt, cupping her breast through the thin fabric of her bra. She arched her back, forcing more of her breast into his grasp. His breathing hitched when she ground her pelvis against his, and she smiled a little in satisfaction. She bit his lip, but didn't realize the mistake until he pulled his mouth away.

"Doing that again would be a mistake, sweetheart." His breath scorched her throat. She could feel the light scrape of his fangs against her flesh and she gulped. "I'm having a very difficult time controlling myself. That would put me right over the edge, so unless you want it rough I suggest you refrain from such contact."

She drew a shaky breath. "What if I want it rough?"

Marco's gaze met hers, searching and fiery at the same time. Finally he rolled off her and back on the mattress. "You don't want rough, at least not my kind of rough."

"You might be surprised." What the hell was she talking about? He'd kidnapped her, and all she could think about was how much she wanted those sharp teeth to sink into her—

Damn it. Now she was the one losing her mind. "You know what? You're right. I don't want it rough. I don't want it from you at all."

He rolled onto his side and played with a lock of her hair. "Liar."

He was right, of course. She was a liar. She wanted him, and she couldn't do anything about it. The only thing that made her feel better was the impressively bulging fly of his pants, which indicated he was in the same situation. She nearly smiled at the thought, but the worried look in his eyes changed her mind. "What's the matter?"

"You have a little blood here." He swiped his hand across her mouth and his fingers came away tinged with blood.

She blinked and licked her lips, tasting the blood for herself. "Sorry. It's not from me. I guess it's yours. It must have happened when I bit your lip."

He ran his hand across his mouth. "Must have." He closed his eyes and took a deep breath, letting it out slowly.

"I didn't mean to hurt you."

He snapped his eyes open. "You didn't hurt *me*."

"What's that supposed to mean?"

"Probably nothing. Forget it. Just watch what you do around me, okay? I *like* pain."

She rubbed her face hard with her hands, trying to hang onto that last, tiny thread of sanity before she ripped all his clothes off and rode him until they were both screaming with pleasure. Finally, sanity prevailed in the form of cleanliness. She could only imagine how terrible she looked right now. Why had he even wanted to touch her?

"You know, I really think I need to take a shower."

He nodded, his expression both pained and relieved. "I suppose you're going to need clean clothes, too."

"Well, that would be nice."

"Okay. I think I can handle this." He walked to the door. "I'll be back in a little while."

Chapter Six

"Wait a minute, you did *what*?" Ellie faced him, her hands on her hips. "Please tell me you're joking."

Marco shrugged. "Nope."

"Well, that's it. I always knew there was something seriously wrong with you. Now I have the proof." Ellie gestured to the bags she'd just dropped on the couch. "It's not too late for me to take these back to the store. You could let her go, and I'll give her a ride back to the city."

"Don't get any ideas." He crossed his arms over his chest. "She's staying."

Ellie shook her head in disbelief. "Amara Daniels is a public personality. Somebody's bound to miss her. Honestly, Marco, you can't just go around kidnapping people because you don't like what they do for a job."

"It's not just that, Ell." He sighed and paced the room. "You wouldn't understand."

She raised an eyebrow at that remark, obviously annoyed. "Oh, no?"

"Well, maybe a little."

Ellie laughed, but she didn't look altogether amused. "A little? I think I know you better than anyone."

She had a point there. Not that he'd ever admit it to her. "Thanks for bringing the stuff, Ell. I owe you one."

"Why do I have a feeling you're going to owe me a lot more by the time you come to your senses and stop trying to scare the poor woman? You're going to let her go home soon, right?"

"Eventually. Just not now." He sighed. "I just need to get this worked out. I've got to get her off my mind."

"And you think holding her captive is going to achieve that?" Ellie stared at him intently. "What the hell is wrong with you? I know you can be a little impulsive at times, but you're breaking the law."

He shoved a hand through his hair. Why *was* he doing this? It had started out as lashing-out in anger, but it was turning into something more. A little more quickly and less smoothly than he would have liked.

"I don't know what's wrong with me, Ell. Maybe I'm finally going crazy."

She shook her head. "No. That happened a long time ago. Do I get to meet her?"

"No."

"Why not?" Ellie glared at him, her blue eyes practically piercing a hole through him. It always freaked him out when she did that, but for the most part he was immune.

Just to be on the safe side, he looked away. "Are you out of your mind?"

"Obviously not as much as you are."

"I can't let you see her right now. Maybe later. Besides, she's probably asleep by now, anyway." He'd left Amara alone for hours again. He just didn't know what to do with her. Taking out his revenge would be so much easier if he could be in the same room with her and not want to take her to bed.

Ellie stood in front of him, her hands on her hips. She cocked her head to the side, probably trying to read more into the situation than what was actually there. He shook his head. "Knock it off. I'm not going to hurt her."

He knew it, and so did Ellie. She'd known him long enough to know he wasn't capable of physically hurting a woman, at least not in a malicious way. Ellie was a friend. She didn't need to know anything about his sex life.

That was the main reason he couldn't keep Amara. Human women tended to get hurt with vampires. It wasn't intentional. In highly physical or emotional situations control was an elusive thing.

Ellie pursed her lips and stared at him for what seemed like an eternity. Finally she sighed heavily. "I hope you know what you're doing."

He laughed. "Of course I do."

No. He didn't. He'd made a stupid mistake, but he didn't want to change it. He *wanted* Amara here, as crazy as this whole thing sounded.

"All right. I guess I should get back to my grandmother before she burns her house down again. Maybe one of these days you can help me convince her to move back to Massachusetts with me. Then I wouldn't have to make so many trips all the way out here." Ellie walked to the door.

"Yeah, I could probably do that. Of course, I'd miss your visits."

"You could always move back, too."

"Nah. I really like California." *Liar*. "I don't want to have to move back and deal with the snow."

Ellie saw right through him. "You just don't want to deal with my family trying to take care of you. I know they can get a little obnoxious, but they really do mean well."

True. There was something about having four grown women fighting over who got to be your surrogate mother that had a guy looking for a place to hide.

"Thanks again for your help, Ellie."

"You know I'd do anything for you. Well, almost." She kissed his cheek. "You know, one of these days I might just collect on one of those favors you owe me. They just keep adding up."

He did owe Ellie a lot. A few times over the years when he'd been hurt, she'd given him a place to stay and helped him recuperate. Not to mention the woman was a miracle worker with computers. She'd helped him with an identity change a time or two. He'd be glad to do anything she needed, just not right now. At the moment, he had his hands full with a strong-willed actress, and he didn't know what to do about her.

Grabbing the shopping bags Ellie had brought, he made his way up to his bedroom where Amara was probably fuming by now. Hours ago, she'd told him she wanted to shower. It wasn't his fault Ellie had taken forever to do the shopping he'd asked her to do.

The woman was lucky Ellie had even been in town. Most of the time she lived in New England, in the same tiny little coastal town where he'd met her years ago. She was only in California occasionally to visit her aging, slightly senile grandmother. If Ellie had been in Stone Harbor instead of California, he would have had a serious problem.

* * * * *

This was just wrong. She'd waited forever, and he still hadn't returned with anything for her to wear. Well, she'd waited as long as she could, and she'd had it with feeling like a disgusting, unclean slime-ball. She'd just have to take a shower first, and wrap up in the sheets or something until he did what he promised.

She stepped into the adjoining bathroom and turned the water on as hot as she could without burning her skin. She stripped, tossing her dirty clothes into the corner of the room. He could pick them up later, assuming he ever decided to come back up here.

She stood under the hot spray, letting the water run over her hair and body. She washed her hair, taking her time, and then hiked the temperature up another notch. It would serve him right if he ran out of hot water, with all he was putting her through.

After at least a half-hour, she turned off the water and got out. She dried off with a big towel and finger-combed her hair the best she could, since she didn't see a brush lying around anywhere. Not wanting to share a toothbrush with a crazy stranger, she squirted toothpaste onto her finger and did the best she could. By the time she was done she felt a tiny bit better, at least until she stepped into the bedroom and a strange wave of dizziness hit her.

She sank down on the bed and took a couple of deep breaths. It was probably going from the steam-filled bathroom to the cooler, dry air in the bedroom that had done it. She'd probably be fine in another minute.

She wasn't. She'd meant to wrap something around her, but she couldn't manage to get her muscles to move. Her arms were leaden and her head felt like it was stuffed with cotton balls. She let her body drop back to the bed, hoping whatever was happening would pass quickly so she could get properly covered up before he came back. This *would* be the time he'd burst through the door, when she was lying naked on his bed and too tired, too boneless to do anything about it.

Lying back on the mattress helped a little. She didn't feel any less dizzy, but at least she didn't have to fight with her body to stay upright. She drew in a couple of deep, slow breaths, but they only served to increase the numb feeling in her limbs. She felt like she'd been sleep-deprived for a week.

She pulled the sheet over her body, knowing she should have gotten dressed in the clothes she had available. Even dirty, they were better than nothing. Instead, she let go, giving in to this strange, new sensation. It was like she was no longer in control of her body—something else was there now, taking her over. She should fight it, but she was too tired to care.

*****

Marco paused in the bedroom door, not sure if he should enter or leave. Amara was reclining on the bed, eyes closed, the sheet draped loosely over her body. The door to the attached bathroom was open, the light on and a towel crumpled on the floor. Apparently she hadn't wanted to wait for clean clothes to take her shower.

Her still-damp hair fanned across the pillow, her natural color a brilliant contrast to the stark white sheets. Her body was firm and toned, yet retained the hourglass figure it was hard to find on women these days. He took a deep breath, remembering a time when women actually coveted a body like Amara's. He missed those times terribly.

Her arm was resting across her chest, the sheet obstructing his view of her ample breasts. He licked his lips, wanting badly to taste her. His pulse sped up at just the thought.

"Are you going to stand there all night, or are you going to come inside?" She startled him when she spoke.

He took a second to gather his control before he responded. "I thought you were sleeping. I have the clothes you asked for."

"I didn't ask. You offered." She sighed, her chest rising and falling with the deep breath. "It's the least you can do, you know, since you're holding me captive and all."

The more he heard it, the more ridiculous it sounded, but he couldn't do anything about that now. He wasn't about to admit he was wrong, at least not in this lifetime.

"Are you okay?" He even surprised himself with his concern for her.

"No. I'm not. Is your shower gel laced with some kind of drug or something?" She spoke slowly, quietly, almost like she'd just woken up.

He shook his head. "I don't know what you're talking about."

"I can't move. I can't think straight. Everything is cloudy." She drew in a ragged breath. "Did you drug me in any way?"

"I wouldn't do that." His reply was harsher than he'd intended. "Are you getting sick?" That was just what he needed right now, on top of everything else—a sick human. "Do you want me to see if I can get you some medicine?"

"For what? The only symptom I have is this tiredness... I can't even explain this. Just forget it." She was silent for a long time before she finally spoke again. "Why me?"

"What do you mean?"

"Why did you choose me? With all those women out there, I should think a good- looking guy like you wouldn't have to resort to kidnapping to get one."

He laughed softly, wondering when his irritation with her had begun mixing with admiration. She was emotionally a lot stronger than he'd imagined. "It was a moment of weakness."

"Weak? Ha! It was more like a moment of being a domineering jerk." Her arm dropped and the sheet slipped from her breasts. His mouth went dry at the sight of her distended nipples. He licked his lips again and fought to keep his fangs retracted. God, what he wouldn't give for a little taste of her right now. Just a tiny bit.

He mentally slammed the door on such thoughts. Amara was not his to taste. She was here to learn, and that was all. *Keep your mind on the goal, buddy. She's not here to be your personal plaything.*

"Do you hate humans or something?"

Her question took him by surprise. He didn't *hate* anything. It was far too strong of a word. "Why would I? I was human once."

"Then why are you doing this?"

He didn't think he liked the answer rattling around in his brain—the one that said it was his quickly growing obsession with her that had driven him to do something insane like kidnap her from her home in the middle of the day.

An obsession with a human woman would be his downfall. He'd seen it happen enough times to know that it almost never ended well. The only hope would be for her to agree to turn—

This train of thought was clearly in need of derailment. He couldn't go on letting the fact that her naked body was right there for his taking distract him. He had to keep his head straight, or she was going to take advantage.

She shifted on the bed. "I'm not going to be making any more of those movies, you know, so this little learning experience of yours is kind of a moot point."

"Why not?"

She sighed again, and he fought the very strong urge to go to her. He lost the battle with his fangs. He wanted so badly to sink them into her neck. Her skin was so smooth and creamy, so inviting…

"I got canned. That's why I'm not doing any more Midnight movies." There was a hitch in her voice and she shivered a little. "I've been looking for another career."

He tried to tell himself he didn't care, but his curiosity got the better of him. "What happened?"

"The producers wanted to capitalize even more on the success of the stupid movies, so they decided to make the next one rated X."

He winced at the thought, but he didn't want to define why. "Oh."

"Yeah, oh. And what's worse is my costar, my ex-fiancé, was all for it. It turns out he got his kicks screwing women on camera, and other men in our bedroom." She laughed, but thought she was on the verge of tears. "So I guess that's it. I suppose you can let me go home now, I no longer need any hands-on training."

The tears she'd been fighting started and he didn't know what to do. He understood a little more now why she hadn't looked at him. "It must kill you to have to be so strong all the time."

"No. I'm fine, really. It's just stress. I never cry."

He believed that. What had happened in her life that made her need to hide her emotions? "Can I get you a glass of water or something?"

"No. Just leave the clothes and go. I'll get dressed in a little while." She rolled to her side, facing the wall instead of him.

He shook his head as he walked across the carpet and climbed into bed with her. He pulled her against him and held her while she cried, the sensations alien to him. Never in his life had he given a woman comfort. Pleasure, of course, in copious amounts. He'd been known to cause a little pain in his time, also, when the situation warranted, but comfort was something new.

Even when he was married, he hadn't been there for his wife. That was the reason she'd given him when she'd told him she'd been with another man. It still hurt to this day to remember her confession, but being here with Amara lessened it inexplicably. She felt *right* in his arms, like she'd been made to rest against him this way. That was ridiculous, considering she was almost four hundred years younger than he was.

Amara stiffened at first, but soon relaxed against him. Her breathing slowed, but she didn't fall asleep. He found himself slowing his breathing to match hers. His palm skimmed over the smooth skin of her stomach and he nuzzled his face in her freshly-washed hair. This actually felt kind of nice. He could get used to this.

Yeah, he could definitely get used to having Amara in his bed. Now that she was relaxed, something other than comfort came to mind. The burning need started low in his abdomen and it was all he could do to ease her into the idea slowly. It was hard to do anything slowly while she was lying naked in his arms. He pushed her hair off her neck and gently stroked the flesh of her throat with his tongue.

That was a mistake. The second he touched her there, his senses went wild. His control snapped, his fangs elongated fully, and his cock hardened impossibly. He sucked in a harsh breath, fighting for a vestige of control, but it was gone. There was nothing he could do about it now. It no longer mattered that she didn't belong to him. In a few moments she would, even if it was just temporary.

He kissed the side of her neck, watching carefully for any signs of protest. When none came, he took her earlobe into his mouth, sucking gently as he scraped his fangs over her skin. She made a soft, whimpering sound that only increased his arousal.

He rested his hand on her hip, drawing her rump back against him. She had to feel his erection pushing against her. He tightened his grip on her hip as his thrust his pelvis against her.

She reached back and grabbed his wrist. He expected her to pull his hand away from her, but she didn't. She held on to him, keeping him there. "Your hands are so warm."

"Did you expect them to be any different?"

She paused. "Well, yeah. I did."

He eased his hand along her hipbone, down her stomach. When he caressed her lower abdomen, she tightened her grip on his wrist. "Stop."

He lowered his mouth back to her ear, licking the tender flesh just beneath it. "Do you want me to stop?"

Her soft moan told him he'd found a very sensitive spot on her body. "No, just...wait."

He held his hand still, but continued to caress the flesh under her ear with the tip of his tongue. After a little while she tilted her head to give him better access. This time when he lowered his hand further down her soft skin, she didn't protest. He skimmed his fingers over her curls before cupping her mound in his hand.

"I need to taste you, Amara."

She stiffened in his arms. "I don't think that would be a good idea."

It sounded like a terrific idea to him. "Are you afraid?"

She made a little sound of disbelief. "Well, yeah. It's not every day that when a man says he wants to taste you he means to literally take a bite."

He let his fangs graze her neck, not breaking the skin, just enough to make her shiver. "It'll be good. I can bring you a lot of pleasure that way."

"Who says I want you to bring me pleasure at all?" She said the words, but her tone told him she was lying.

"Don't you?"

She breathed deeply. "I...I guess I do. I'm still shaky. I don't know what I want."

In this state, hovering between fatigue and arousal, she'd be very easy to sway. He wasn't proud of the fact that he was willing to try, but he wanted her badly. If she truly wanted him to stop, he would, but he'd have to hear the words. His slipped his fingers past her folds, stroking her clit gently. His touch was soft, designed to make her crazy with lust but not give her what she needed for relief. It worked. Soon her hand, still gripping his wrist, was trying to push him harder against her. He pulled his hand away completely, and she sighed.

He removed her hand from his wrist, pulling it back and settling it on his thigh. He nudged a knee between her legs, raising her top leg higher as he slid his hand between her legs again.

He clamped his mouth onto her neck, suckling the skin hard while he slipped a finger into her wet cunt. He stroked in and out of her rhythmically, thumbing her clit at the same time. He brought her right to the edge of orgasm before he pulled his hand away again.

"Why did you stop?"

"You need something from me. I need something from you, too."

She shook her head. "No. I don't want you to hurt me."

He smiled against her skin. "There won't be any pain. I promise you that." His teeth grazed her flesh, nipping enough to just barely break the skin. She cried out and he brought his hand to her breast, his fingers circling her nipple. She squirmed against him as he warred with the primitive instincts taking control of his body. He wanted to ravish her, but something stopped him. She needed him to take it slowly, and he would do that for her as long as he could.

Never in his life had he fought so hard for control of himself. It didn't take much to push him over the edge. A tiny drop of blood formed at the wound he'd inflicted, and it made him wild. Rolling her nipple between his thumb and fingers, he sank his fangs fully into the delicate skin of her neck.

She let out a breath that ended with a moan. "*Oh God.*"

He echoed her sentiments. She would never know what he was feeling. Every sensation she felt, he felt tenfold. And he was still completely dressed.

The taste of her blood in his mouth was enough to do him in. He felt her pulse beating under his lips and her body thrum with energy against his. She was close to coming and it wouldn't take much to send her over the edge.

He stroked her labial lips, spreading her folds. She arched against him when he slid his finger back into her dripping cunt. She was so hot, so wet, that he couldn't wait to have her. Tonight he would. There was no doubt about that in his mind now. She was pliant, willing in his arms. He could do with her as he pleased.

His cock hardened way past the point of pain. After he finished feeding, he was going to have to get inside her. There was no choice. It simply had to be done, or he wouldn't get any sleep again. Ever.

She tasted better than any woman he'd sampled. His body heaved and he suckled her hard. He couldn't get enough of her, in any way. The woman was pure fire under his touch, and when he was this close he ignited, too.

She writhed against him as he slid a finger into her cunt. One stroke of his finger and she came. Her bucking against him was nearly his undoing. The only thing that stopped him from potentially hurting her was the fact that, despite the strength she'd shown, she seemed so fragile next to him. That, and the very scary realization Amara Daniels could very well be his mate.

With one last sip of her blood, he pulled away from her and rolled to his back. In over four hundred years, both as a mortal and a vampire, he hadn't found the one woman he was destined to be with. He'd thought he had, twice, but both times were mistakes. He'd given up hope so many years ago he couldn't remember exactly when.

Amara was human. Not just a human, but a skeptical human. That was the worst kind. She couldn't possibly be the woman for him. He would just have to ignore the fact that something about their being together felt right. He was loathe to call it destiny, since destiny wouldn't dictate he kidnap a woman to get her attention.

"That was...wow." Her voice was breathless as she rolled over and rested her head on his chest. He could feel her body still trembling from his assault. "But what about you?"

"I'm fine." That was possibly the biggest lie of his life. If she so much as touched him, he would explode. He couldn't risk hurting her. In fact, first thing in the morning he was going to return her to where she belonged.

Far away from him.

Her hand skimmed over his chest and down to the waistband of his pants. He reached for her hands, but she shooed him away. "What do you want, Marco?"

"I think I should leave you alone so you can get some sleep." If she touched him, he would *have* to fuck her. There was no debating the matter. If he fucked her, he would have to take more of her blood. He wouldn't be able to resist. But he wouldn't hurt her either. He'd taken a lot, and he didn't know how much more he could take before it affected her.

He tried to sit up, but she pushed him back down. "Lay still for a second, will you?"

"Amara, stop. This isn't a good idea. You're going to need your rest after what I took from you."

She brought her hand to her throat and touched the fading marks from his fangs. She swallowed hard, but she smiled. "You didn't hurt me. Not too much."

"I told you I wouldn't."

"Yeah, well with you I never know what to believe."

The rasp of his zipper caught his attention. He looked down as she started to slide his pants off his legs.

"Get undressed, would you? I don't want to wait much longer. "

He would have laughed if he hadn't been so turned on. She'd managed to distract him enough to start undressing him without his notice. That was a first for him.

Before he could think about the consequences, he stripped off the remainder of his clothes. Amara's skin was flushed with desire, and he could see from her eyes she plainly wanted him. He was a little confused. Usually the human women just fell asleep. He couldn't believe she wanted to be satisfied again already.

Or that she'd thought about him as well as herself.

"Are you sure this is what you want?" He asked. "I don't want any regrets later."

She nodded. "I want this. You have no idea how much I want this. Now shut up for a minute, okay?"

Who was he to argue with that?

She grasped his cock in her palm and her touch was like fire shooting through him. She was so warm everywhere. He let her stroke him for a minute or two, until he couldn't stand it anymore. Then he gently removed her hand and rolled her onto her back. He would take her gently the first time. *And it would probably kill him.* Anything beyond that...well he couldn't be held responsible for his actions.

He paused for a brief moment and caught her gaze. "I have to know one thing before we take this any further. Are you protected?"

"If by protected you mean birth control, then yes. I get a shot every three months." She frowned, scrunching up her nose. "Is that your concern?"

"Yes. I don't need to worry about diseases. My immune system is too strong to be affected by them or to carry them. But pregnancy is another matter altogether."

"A vampire can still procreate?"

She really had a lot to learn. "Yes. It's difficult with a human, but definitely not unheard of."

"Well, I'm all set so there's nothing to worry about." Her voice was barely above a whisper, but it held a husky quality.

He moved between her legs and positioned the head of his engorged cock at the entrance of her cunt. He paused, watching her carefully for a last-minute objection. When he found none, he slid his cock all the way into her. She moaned softly, rolling her head back against the pillow.

For a long moment, he couldn't move. She felt so hot and tight, so *right*, that he wanted to savor the sensation. She looked up at him through half-lidded eyes, her expression filled with desire and tenderness.

He didn't want her tenderness. He didn't deserve it, not after what he'd done to her. But he'd take it, and anything else she had to offer him tonight. He couldn't possess her like he wanted to, but at least they'd have a little while before she left him to go back to her real life.

He couldn't remember the last time he'd slept with a woman he actually cared about. It had been hundreds of years since he'd allowed himself to care in that way. Amara could change all that, if he'd let her. He didn't plan on it.

Her moans of protest finally goaded him to move. With each stroke, staying in control of his primal side, the part of him that was more animal than human, got more and more difficult. He wanted to ravish her in every possible way, mark her so that she would know she was his forever.

But he would *not* hurt her. The more he repeated that, the harder it got to stick to it. And if she kept digging her nails into his back like that, he was going to do something they'd both regret. He suckled her breasts, laving her puckered nipples until she whimpered.

"More," she cried when he pulled his mouth away.

He trailed his tongue along her collarbone, up her throat, across her jaw. She tasted like soft, clean woman, a mix of sensual and innocent—a flavor that left him reeling. He nipped her neck gently in several places, earning another few scratches along his back.

She raised her chin, exposing her neck like an offering. As much as he'd like to sink his teeth back into her, he couldn't. Not yet, when he'd so recently fed from her. And definitely not when he was so short on willpower. He'd never intentionally hurt her, but accidents had been known to happen in these situations.

She apparently sensed his reservations. "Let go, Marco. Please. I need everything from you."

She arched her back and dug her nails into his sides, shattering the last of his control. With a savage groan he pounded into her, each stroke harder than the last, no longer caring about anything but being inside her and the pleasure her body brought to all of his senses.

He sank his teeth into her neck again, needing just one more taste of her. It was a very integral part of his climax, and it would also increase the intensity of Amara's. He knew she felt the change right away by the hitch in her breath.

She met him thrust for thrust, arching her back and clawing at him in a very feline way. She screamed when she came, her nails scratching him deeply enough to draw blood. He knew she'd left welts in his skin and the pain was enough to send him over the edge into his own climax, his hot seed spurting inside her.

He collapsed on top of her, too spent to move. He groaned against the warm flesh of her neck. Amara wriggled against him and sighed contentedly. She ran her hand down his back, stopping when she found the scratches she'd left.

"Did I really cut you that badly?"

He rolled onto his back. "It's no big deal. I've been cut worse in my lifetime."

"Yeah, but I didn't want to hurt you."

"Sometimes a little pain can be a good thing." Actually, it'd been more like a lot of pain, but he wasn't going to tell her that yet.

Her breathing was still a little heavy, which didn't surprise him. In fact, she should have been exhausted by now. He certainly was. "Are you okay?"

She laughed. "Why wouldn't I be? I just had the best sex of my life."

He nodded, in total agreement. Who would have thought he'd be so compatible with a woman he'd kidnapped? "Are you feeling okay?"

"Sure. I feel like I'm floating somewhere above the bed." She laughed a little. "I'll let you know when I come back down."

He couldn't help himself. He smiled at her honest, open manner. "You should sleep for a while. You're going to need it."

"I'm okay." She yawned. "I guess I am a little tired."

He leaned down and kissed the top of her head, listening to her breathing finally slow. In no time, she was asleep. She needed the rest a lot more than he did. If he was any kind of a man he'd walk away now before things got even more complicated.

Unfortunately for her, he'd never claimed to be chivalrous. At his best, he was arrogant, greedy, and self-centered. He made sure he always got what he wanted, and right now, for some strange reason, he wanted to *cuddle*. That was another new thing for him, but he was going to go with it while he had the chance. He'd berate himself for it later, he was sure of it, but he'd enjoy what he could get for now.

He never stayed the night, or the day if that was the case, but he could make an exception for Amara since she was in his bed. He wrapped her in his arms and joined her in sleep.

Chapter Seven

Amara woke up alone some time later. The side of the bed where Marco had been was warm. He hadn't been gone long. She stretched, her entire body stiff from their lovemaking.

Or was it just sex? It had felt a lot more complicated and emotional than that, but she didn't know how Marco felt. She blinked, her senses slowly returning. She didn't know Marco at all. She'd just had wild, out of control, totally uninhibited sex with a complete stranger. Okay, she'd really lost it now.

Not that it really mattered, the man was a vampire. She had no future with someone who was a different...well, she still wasn't sure how to describe what he was, except that he drank blood.

She was no longer certain about the undead part. He definitely had a heartbeat. She'd felt it pounding right along with hers. He breathed—his breath had been hot and erotic against her sensitive neck. Heck, if the man could procreate then he had to be alive in some form.

Alive or not, it didn't change the fact that her lover was a vampire. Believing that was still a stretch, even after he'd drunk her blood. *That* was a feeling she could get used to. She'd never come so hard in her life. Her clit still ached. Her vulva throbbed. In fact, if he were still in bed with her she probably would have jumped him without a second thought.

Did he feel what she had? Was his climax as strong as hers, or was she just another fuck for him? If he'd stayed, she could have asked. Where had he slunk off to in the middle of the night—day—whatever it was. She'd spent so much time in this room she'd lost track of *when* she was.

He'd enjoyed himself. He'd probably deny it later like a typical male, but he'd had just as good a time as she had. Maybe better. *Take that, Derek*! No more boring Amara in the bedroom. Marco seemed to bring out her wild side. Maybe she owed it to herself, and her next lover, to fully explore this new set of possibilities. If Marco was willing, she was definitely able.

What was it like for him to drink her blood? The thought of tasting someone's blood had always turned her off, but now she was a little curious. Marco had felt so good inside her. Did feeding off of her increase his pleasure? Would she feel the same if she...

Wait a second. Was she going mental? *Humans did not drink blood.* Humans didn't *think* about drinking blood. Well, not unless they had some serious mental issues. She was human, therefore it was not okay for her to fantasize about drinking Marco's blood.

End of discussion.

Where was he, anyway? She got out of bed and rummaged through the bags he'd left on the floor. Pulling out a pair of jeans and a sweatshirt, she got dressed. The clothes were a little bit baggy, but it was better than putting on the dirty stuff she'd stripped out of before her shower.

She was surprised that when she tested the doorknob, the door swung open. Hmm. He'd left it unlocked. Did that mean she was free to roam about his house? Or did he just want her to go home? Maybe he'd changed his mind about keeping her here now that he found out she was so easy.

She groaned. What an impression he must have of her. She didn't usually jump into bed with a guy she'd just met. Her only excuse was that she'd been under a lot of stress lately. She'd finally snapped.

The downstairs of the house was dim, the only source of light a few wall sconces. The walls were dark beige only a few shades lighter than the hardwood floors. Antiques made up the majority of the decor, stuff he'd probably been collecting for years. A lot of it he'd probably bought new.

That was a scary thought.

She wandered into the kitchen and got a glass of water. She drank it down quickly, but winced at the oddly metallic taste it left in her mouth. The clock on the stove read eleven o'clock, and the sky was black beyond the kitchen window. That meant she'd slept through an entire day.

How did that happen? She normally lived on a few hours' sleep every night. When did she get to be so lazy that she slept for nearly twenty-four hours without blinking an eye?

The back door was cracked open, the sound of crickets filling the night air. She pulled the door open all the way and stepped outside. Marco was sitting on a wooden bench on the deck. He glanced up when he saw her, and for the first time he actually smiled. "Did you sleep well?"

She nodded. "I guess. Why did you let me sleep so long?"

He shrugged. "You needed your rest. I had no right to take blood from you."

"If I didn't want you to, I would have said no." She sat down next to him, her leg brushing against his knee. She tried not to let him see that even the small touch affected her, but she was learning there wasn't much she could keep from him.

"You didn't want to be kidnapped. That didn't stop me."

She rolled her eyes. "This is new. The big, bad alpha-vamp is actually showing remorse."

"Don't start." The warning tone was plain in his voice.

"What are you going to do, bite me?" She raised an eyebrow in challenge. "I have to warn you, though, I liked it."

He shook his head and laughed. "You were supposed to."

"Is it always like that?"

"Pleasurable? Yes, unless I deliberately choose to make it painful. During sex, the pleasure it brings is incomparable. How else would we be able to get anyone to agree to it?" He paused. "But like it was between us, that was unusual. It's not always so strong."

"But it is, sometimes?" She was getting worried. What she'd felt was almost too intense to bear.

"Once in a while."

"How often?"

Marco sighed. "I don't remember the last time it was so good. Is that what you wanted to hear?"

She shook her head. No, it was the exact opposite of what she wanted to hear. She could deal with good. Hell, she could deal with great. But earth-shattering was another matter entirely. She didn't know how to handle her feelings when she knew nothing could ever come of them. Besides the obvious differences in lifespans, she knew practically nothing about him. She still wasn't sure if she wanted to stay, but the thought of another round of his particular brand of sex made it tempting.

"I suppose you want to go now." He didn't look happy about it. *Good.* Perhaps it was his turn for a couple of lessons.

"I'll think about it."

He looked surprised, but he covered it quickly. Heaven forbid the man show a little emotion beyond anger or annoyance.

The more she thought about it, the more she considered staying for a couple of days. Being here with Marco was certainly better than sitting around in her townhouse, waiting for the bills to pile up while she was unable to get another job. She'd rather be here for a little while than out waiting tables at some sleazy restaurant again.

His expression cleared. He'd come to a decision. "There's nothing to think about. You're not going anywhere."

Well, staying sounded like a good idea until he opened his big mouth. Who did he think he was, trying to force her into it? If she did anything, it would be of her own free will. "You left the door unlocked."

"My bedroom door. *Just* the bedroom door. The outside doors will remain locked unless I'm with you."

She shook her head. "Wait a second, after last night you're still going to keep me prisoner here?"

He nodded. "That was the whole point of bringing you here. This isn't a social excursion."

She took a deep breath and counted to ten, trying to control the urge to punch him. Why was it so difficult for him to admit he'd had a good time? "I explained to you that I'm done with those movies. What more do you want from me?"

"What would you do if I let you go now? Would you run to your friends, the tabloids, and tell them about me? I put myself, and a lot of others, at risk when I told you what I really am. I have to know I can trust you before I let you go."

"Please. I live on the outskirts of L.A. Do you know how many psychos there are running around thinking they're vampires?" she asked. "Besides, what makes you think you can't trust me? You barely even know me."

"That's exactly why I need to keep you here for a little while longer. Trust is a very hard thing to earn, especially when I get the feeling you're looking for a way to escape."

"Can you read minds or something?"

He laughed. "No. I can't read minds. For some reason, though, I'm in tune to you."

She was in tune to him also, but she wasn't going to share that knowledge just yet. It might be something she could use later, unless he decided to stop trying to control her life. "So you're going to keep me here, against my will, until you feel you can learn to trust me?"

"Are you really here against your will?"

She had to think about that one. On the one hand, she would do anything to get free. On the other hand, what would she go back to? She had no life, no job, and no friends that weren't interested in her money. What was left?

Marco. And what a hell of a consolation prize he was.

He continued. "Consider this a vacation in the surreal. Relax and enjoy yourself. When I send you home, feel free to alert the authorities. Trust me on this—they will never find me."

And she'd be all alone. As uncertain as she was about him and what they had going on, she didn't like the thought of never seeing him again. "What would you do if I left?"

"Move on. It's what I always do, when I've been some place for too long."

"You'd just leave? Just like that? No goodbyes to anyone?"

"I don't have many close friends. It's just not a safe thing for me to do." He got up from the table and walked to the deck railing, staring out into the blackness of the night. "The few friends I have understand my situation. Ellie, the woman who brought your clothes, is probably the only one I'd miss. But I never stay away from her for long."

Ellie? Jealousy rose in her, confusing her. She had no claim to Marco. She didn't *want* to claim him in any way. Right? He'd *kidnapped* her. He came into her house and took her, brought her here and locked her in his bedroom for days on end.

And he was the best lover she'd *ever* had. That had to count for something. At least it did to her. She didn't know anything about his sexual practices. For all she knew, vampires had wild orgies all the time.

"Who is Ellie?" She spoke slowly, not sure if she really wanted his answer.

Marco laughed. He turned from the railing and walked over to her. "Are you a little worried?"

She shook her head quickly. "Of course not. I'm just…curious."

"Curious." He took a deep breath. "Ellie is a close friend, and nothing more. In some ways she's like a little sister to me. In others, she's more like a mother hen. It's a complicated relationship, one I'll explain some other time. You've heard enough for a while, I think."

"So you two never…"

"Ellie and I have never slept together. We never will, either."

Maybe she was a hideous beast. She smiled, feeling a little better. "Oh. Is Ellie a vampire, too?"

He shook his head. "No, Ellie is not a vampire. But she is the only woman I've ever met who understands me."

That remark stung. "I understand you."

He raised a brow. "Do you? I don't think so."

She waved a hand in the air. "Please. You're not that hard to understand. When you want something, you take it. You don't ask, because that would be a sign of weakness. Women have no place in your life, except as toys. When you get mad, you act first and worry about the consequences later. You're impulsive, arrogant, and feel like you're entitled to whatever you want. Thinking about the other people involved is secondary."

She cocked her head to the side and waited for his response. He said nothing.

"Don't bother to deny it, because I can see in your eyes how right I am." She shook her head. "And believe me, it has nothing to do with you being a vampire. That just seems to be a group of traits most men have."

"You paint me in a very bad light, woman."

She shrugged. "All men are the same. What can I say?"

"Although you're right about quite a bit, us lowly males do have some good qualities, too."

"And what would those be?" She had yet to see them. Even the ones she thought she could trust, like Robby, turned on her eventually.

She wasn't even going to get started on Derek. To think, she'd actually planned on marrying the guy. She was glad that she'd told him he had to wear a condom for extra protection until after the wedding. Who knows what kind of diseases she might have picked up, since he'd apparently slept with just about everyone he'd ever met.

"You're just going to have to find that out on your own. It won't be too hard, if you're really interested in looking." He walked back inside, stopping by the fridge. "Are you hungry?"

"A little." She followed him. "Why don't you tell me about some of your good points? I'm beginning to wonder if you have any."

"I can cook. What do you want to eat?"

"Marco—"

He held up a hand to stop her. "Let me cook you some breakfast first. We can talk after."

"Supper. It's after eleven. Almost time for a midnight snack."

He shrugged. "That all depends on how you look at it. Do you want eggs? Toast?"

She snorted. "Not at this time of night. I have enough trouble forcing that stuff down at six in the morning. It's nighttime. I want a cheeseburger."

"A cheeseburger?" He blinked a few times. "Are you sure that's what you want?"

"Yes." If she was going to be on vacation, she was going to enjoy herself. She no longer had to live on a piece of lettuce and a couple of carrot sticks a day so she could fit into her skimpy costumes or conform to Hollywood's twisted version of beauty. Now she could eat like a human and not someone's pet rabbit. "Please?"

He looked shocked, but he relented. "Okay. I'll see what I can do."

*****

Marco watched as Amara finished off the last of the cheeseburger. He was a little astounded when she'd requested something so simple. She was most likely used to gourmet meals. Why would she want something she could get at any fast food restaurant in the country?

She enjoyed it, though. The little noises she made while eating it rivaled the ones she'd made last night in bed. His mouth went dry just listening to her.

He was glad he'd had Ellie bring in some food, or else Amara would have starved. He'd learned firsthand she wouldn't eat peanut butter, and that was about the only thing he ever kept in the cabinets.

She looked different sitting across from him at the kitchen table than she did in the films, or even at the functions where he'd seen her. Now she looked more relaxed, more natural, and less like the snotty bitch he'd thought she was. He was learning a lot about her, and what he learned scared him. He had less and less reason to hate her with every sentence that came out of her mouth.

In fact, he was disgusted to find he was actually starting to like her.

Wanting her body was one thing, but truly admiring who she was as a person was out of the question. At this rate, the woman was going to turn him into a softie by the end of the week.

"Tell me where you get your insight into my true nature."

She shrugged and finished off the last of the burger. "Growing up, my mother got married to a different man every other year. I had seven stepfathers and quite a few *uncles*. I learned a lot just watching them."

"You don't have a very high opinion of men, do you?"

She snorted. "Are you kidding? Why should I? Every single man in my life has proven to be a gigantic letdown."

Maybe she just hadn't found the right man yet.

"Where do you get off, asking a question like that?" she continued, her expression irritated. "Your opinion of women seems pretty low."

"Yeah, and I have a good reason for that, too."

"What's that?"

He studied her, debating how much to tell her. If he relayed the entire story, he'd scare her off for good. Then again, that would certainly solve the problem of unwanted emotional attachments.

"I was married once. A very long time ago."

"Okay."

"My wife was not exactly what you'd call faithful." He took a deep breath, the pain of what had happened still there, even though it had dulled to a low throb.

"I'm sorry."

She truly looked it, too. And he was sorry for what he was about to say to her, but there was no way to do it gently. "Do you want to know why I'm a vampire?"

She nodded, but she didn't look so sure.

"I was to be executed for killing my wife and her lover."

"You were *what?*"

"You heard me right the first time. I'm not going to repeat myself. I was convicted of killing the two of them, but before I could be hanged my wife's father took matters into his own hands and stabbed me. There just happened to be a vampire living in our village. I guess the smell of my blood must have been quite an enticement for him. He came to me and offered me a way I could live in exchange for a meal."

"The rest is quite a long story, and I don't need to go into the sordid details, but I think you need to know exactly what I am."

She licked her lips and he had the sudden urge to suck them into his mouth. He shook his head to remind himself he was trying to push her away, not draw her closer.

He watched her closely, waiting for that mental retreat he knew was inevitable. It never came.

"I see. But that doesn't answer the question of how you became a vampire."

He blew out a breath. He'd anticipated fear, almost welcomed it, but not her curiosity. "I explained how I came to be what I am. What more do you need to know?"

"Not who, Marco, *how*. How does it happen? Did he make you feed off of him?"

She sat on the edge of her seat, waiting for his answer. He didn't like her eagerness.

"Why do you need to know the technical details?"

"I don't need to. I want to."

He pushed away from the table. "Maybe sometime I'll tell you. But not tonight."

She'd be surprised at how simple it really was. There was no way he was going to arm her with that kind of knowledge. Before she could protest, he stalked out of the room.

Chapter Eight

Men!

Just when you think you're getting somewhere with them, they get all closed-mouthed and cranky.

Amara finished the last of the dishes, which Marco hadn't even bothered to help with, and laid the towel neatly on the counter to dry. She'd asked a perfectly reasonable question. Was it too much for her to expect an answer in the same night? She didn't think so, but apparently the dark and brooding one had other ideas.

Oh, well. His loss. If he didn't want to talk to her, fine. But he'd better not be expecting any bedtime privileges until he learned to stop being such a jerk.

She settled on the couch with the remote, finally deciding on the late night news. With three channels to choose from, the choice wasn't exactly difficult.

He wanted her to consider this a vacation. Well, it certainly wasn't her fantasy vacation. In her fantasy, she would be on a tropical island, *alone*, with not a single man in sight to mess up her plans. She'd spend the days soaking up the sun and the evenings relaxing on a hammock on the front porch of her bungalow.

Without an annoying male to bring down the mood.

She would most certainly *not* be trapped in the middle of nowhere, locked in a house where the only company was a man who changed moods as often as she washed her hair.

She couldn't stand this anymore. After living most of her life in noisy trailer parks and then L.A., she needed some kind of noise. Another couple of days here and she was going to be as crazy as Marco was.

She got up from the couch and walked to the front door. She jiggled the doorknob a few times, but couldn't get the door to open. She jiggled harder, ready to break it down if she had to. For God's sake, the man didn't even have a stereo, at least not one she could find. She *had* to get some noise in her life.

She was considering putting her fist through the glass inset when a hand closed around hers and she nearly jumped out of her skin.

"Are you going somewhere, Amara?" Marco's voice was a low growl and his breath hot against her skin. A little too hot. He was angry.

Oops.

She winced. "I, uh…"

"You expect me to trust you, when the second I let you out of my sight you try to leave?" His hands came up to cup her breasts. "Were you even going to say goodbye?"

She shook her head. No goodbyes for this girl, not ever. She preferred clean breaks. Not that she'd be able to break away from Marco, not completely anyway. He was the kind of man who burrowed himself under a woman's skin for life. She wondered if he was ever planning to let her go.

"Are you afraid of me?"

"No." But she was now. Just a little. It was that confession that had done it. He'd killed his wife, and her lover. That was something she wouldn't easily forget. No matter how good he was in bed, the man was capable of murder.

He was a vampire. Weren't they all capable of the senseless destruction of human life? Or was that just in the movies? Reality wasn't the same as it used to be.

"Why do you insist on lying to me?" He nipped her earlobe. "I can tell you aren't being truthful."

He turned her around to face him, pushing her back into the door. "Do you really think I would let you go this easily?"

She shrugged, trying for casual. "A girl can hope, can't she?"

"You want to leave?"

The funny thing with that was, if he wasn't holding her hostage she wouldn't mind getting to know him a little better. Being kidnapped kind of took the fun out of it. "It doesn't matter what I want. You aren't giving me any choice."

For just a second, he actually looked upset. But he covered it quickly. "We all have choices."

"And the one you made when you brought me here wasn't exactly a sane one."

He sighed, his eyes closing briefly. "I told you why I did that."

Yeah. He'd been telling her his reason since he brought her here. It was starting to lose its edge. "You have yet to tell me exactly what you plan on doing to me."

"I haven't decided that myself." He pulled her up against him. "I thought I'd start with this."

His mouth crushed hers in a kiss that was anything but gentle. He forced his tongue into her mouth as his teeth grazed her lips and his body pressed against hers. When he released her, he looked as shaken as she did. This time he didn't even try to hide it.

A man had never looked at her quite like that before. She'd seen lust, heat, amusement, and boredom—sometimes all in the same night. But this was a first for her. This wasn't about sex. Well, it wasn't *entirely* about sex. Marco wanted *her*, not a warm body to sink into every night. He hadn't gone looking for someone else last night after they'd had sex. Actually, he'd given her pleasure and didn't even ask for anything in return. She'd never met a man like that in her life.

Maybe this could be more of a vacation than she thought.

After what Derek had put her through, she deserved a man who would put her needs first. She deserved a little pampering, a little fun, and who better to give her what she needed than Marco? If she could just forget about the whole kidnapper-captive problem, she'd be fine.

"Would you really continue to hold me here against my will, even if I really wanted to leave?" She asked him.

He said nothing, but the look in his eyes told her all she needed to know. He felt guilty for what he'd done, even if he couldn't own up to it. She looped her arms around his neck and pulled him down for another kiss.

He seemed surprised, but he got over it quickly. He had her back against the door almost immediately, his hands all over her body. She squirmed against him, knowing she was torturing him and loving every second of it.

Marco ran his hands up her sides until he was once again cupping her breasts. She moaned as the tips of his fingers skimmed her nipples, making them instantly hard. Her panties were soaked in a matter of seconds.

He was so close that she could feel his heartbeat against her chest. She ran her hands along his abdomen, admiring the hard ridges of muscle under his shirt. She dragged her fingernails over his waist, eliciting a low groan from him.

He grabbed her hands and pulled them away from his body when she reached for the waistband of his pants. "Why are you doing this to me? Are you *trying* to kill me?"

"Don't you like it when I touch you?" She struggled against his hold, finally able to pull her hands away.

"That's not what I mean." He paused and drew a deep breath as her fingers skimmed over his fly. "I don't know what's going on here. One minute you want to stay, the next you're trying to sneak out the door."

She hardly knew Marco. He had yet to give her a last name. She'd known Derek for five years before she'd accepted his proposal, and he turned out to be someone different than she'd thought.

"I'll stay, for now. But only if you promise not to lock me in the bedroom anymore. I was so bored I was ready to pull out my hair."

He raised an eyebrow. "You weren't up there for *that* long."

"I have a very short attention span."

"I'll keep that in mind." He kissed her hard and fast, his hands working on ridding her of her pants. He cupped her mound in his palm, his thumb skimming through her curls. He separated her folds with his fingers and lightly played with her clit.

Her knees nearly gave out right then and there. She clutched his shoulders to keep from falling. His touch was like a brand on her sensitive flesh. His fingertips seared right through her until the sensations consumed her and there was nothing left but the two of them. She angled her hips against his hand to give him better access.

Forget going upstairs. What was wrong with right here? The door seemed sturdy enough. "Marco, please."

He leaned his forehead against hers, his breathing ragged. "Please, what? What do you want, Amara? Do you want me to stop? This is the last time I'm going to ask. I don't want you to feel like this is an obligation, because it's not. It has to be what you want. It's your choice, but you've got to make it quickly."

She shook her head. "No. I'd die if you stopped." She almost believed that she would. If he stopped touching her, she felt like her heart might give out. She needed this, she needed him. She'd probably look back on this whole thing and wonder if she'd been insane, but it would be well worth it.

"Upstairs..."

"No." She shook her head. "*Now!*"

He stripped off her remaining clothes and dropped them next to the door. Her bare back touched the cold glass of the inset and she shivered. The cool, smooth glass behind her coupled with his warm, rough hands proved more arousing than she would have ever imagined. At the same time, she felt entirely too exposed to the world.

She'd done some wild things in her younger days, but nothing compared to this. There was a big difference between throwing a couple of keg parties and having practically nonstop sex with an immortal kidnapper.

"The window…someone will see."

"No one is anywhere near here. We're all alone."

This coming from a man who lived his life in relative seclusion and had no idea how far the press would go to get pictures. She'd lived that life for the past ten years. It wasn't exactly fun.

Then again, maybe something like this was just what she needed to jumpstart her sagging career. Sagging? Ha! It was more like it was completely dead, rotting away on the side of an old dirt road. Still, scandals worked for other Hollywood types. Why not her?

She could see the headlines now—"Washed Up Starlet Kidnapped" by Crazy Vampire and Forced to Have Sex in Semi-Public Places.

That wasn't right. First, she wasn't really a starlet. Sure, she had her fans, but the circles were relatively small. It was more of a cult following, really.

Second, if she ran around screaming that a vampire had kidnapped her, she'd be committed.

Third, he wasn't *forcing* her into anything. Everything they did, she walked into consensually. It helped that he was so sexy it made her wet to just look at him.

He didn't even bother to undress himself, he just lowered his zipper and released his cock. He lifted her legs and wrapped them around his waist, thrusting his cock into her cunt. He pulled her down hard, impaling her completely. She moaned and clung on to him, letting him control the pace of his thrusts. She was already close to orgasm, the intensely pleasurable sensations hovering just out of her reach. She tried to hold herself off, wanting to savor everything about the moment.

She kissed his shoulder and licked the skin of his jaw. Near the pulse in his neck she paused, her mouth watering. She could almost swear she heard the blood beating in his veins just below the surface of his skin. She wet her lips with the tip of her tongue and her pulse kicked up a few notches. She closed her eyes and inhaled deeply, almost believing she could *smell* his blood. It wouldn't take a lot of effort to get to it. All that warm blood, so close...

Shit. Was she going to think about acting like him every time they had sex? She could go for a little biting, but actually wanting to draw blood was a little strange, even for her.

The friction of Marco's thick cock sliding in and out of her cunt, her clit rubbing against him in such an enticing way, brought on her orgasm much sooner than she would have liked. She came hard, her body melting into his as she clawed at him and begged for more. Wave after wave of fire burned through her until she thought she couldn't take it anymore.

He came soon after, his body stiffening as he pressed her tightly against the door. He nipped her neck, but didn't go any further than that. She lifted her chin to expose her neck, silently begging him for more. He kissed her throat gently, but pulled away. Instead of giving her what she really wanted, he set her back down on her feet. "If you give me a minute to catch my breath, we could take this upstairs to a more comfortable place."

She nodded. "Mmm."

He smiled wickedly. "Good. I still haven't tasted you yet tonight. I can't go a second without thinking how incredible your flavor is."

A thrill ran through her when she remembered the last time he'd fed off her. She'd been scared, but if she'd known it was *that* good she would have found a vampire lover a hell of a lot sooner. She didn't look forward to going back to the real world and finding a mortal lover.

"Is the feeding a necessary part for you?"

"Not all the time. Sometimes." He paused and looked down at her. "Does it bother you?"

Was he out of his mind? "No. I just wondered."

"You seem to be doing a lot of that lately."

"I guess."

Now that she thought about it, she had. Where had this sudden curiosity come from? Probably it had a little bit to do with the fact that she'd played a vampire for so long, and according to Marco, had been doing it all wrong. Some small part of her had actually become Midnight Morris, and it hurt in a way to have that part of her challenged.

She also wanted to be able to understand Marco. He was a mystery to her, and she somehow felt connected to him. She wanted to learn all she could about what he was.

Or maybe she was just spending way too much time with no one for company but a cranky vampire. His habits were growing on her. She shook her head, thinking that when this was over they'd probably *both* need to be committed.

Marco picked her up and carried her upstairs to his bedroom. "I want to stay with you tonight. All night."

She nodded. There was no sense denying how she felt. She wanted him here, he wanted to be here. Whatever problems they had with each other, they didn't extend into the bedroom.

That was a good thing, because she'd never met a man who could make her come so hard and yet not act like he was king of the world. She hated to admit it, but the conflict made things interesting.

She'd had so much conflict growing up that she'd started to thrive on it. The past couple of years she hadn't had much. Everyone in her life went out of their way to agree with what she said. Well, they had up until the whole porn movie bit. She had started to miss the tension, in some sick and demented way. With Marco, there was conflict abounding in spades. She enjoyed it a lot more than she'd ever tell him.

He nipped her shoulder as he settled her into the mattress. She shivered.

"Are you cold?"

She shook her head. Not even close. She was burning up.

Every nerve in her body felt scorched, and she was afraid she would never recover. She felt the sting of Marco's fangs at the same time she felt his cock push into her cunt. The sensations drove her over the edge into another shattering climax. There was something about those teeth piercing her skin…she couldn't describe it, but the pleasure was unmatched by anything she'd ever experienced.

She clung to him helplessly, her entire body quivering. The tremors washed over her, made more intense by the feeling of his hard shaft sliding in and out of her body. She wrapped her legs around his waist and dug her heels into his buttocks, trying to draw him even closer. He responded with a growl, lifting her rear with his hand and thrusting even deeper.

His muscles tensed and bunched under her hands and his suckling at her throat grew harder. She tilted her chin as high as she could, letting him take what he wanted. Too soon, he stopped. He released her neck, trailing a path of open mouthed kisses from her throat to her collarbone, and finally to her breasts. He nipped the sensitive skin gently before taking one distended nipple into his mouth.

She moaned as the feel of his hot, wet mouth sent her into a series of soft, tiny climaxes that only made her burn for more. Her inner muscles clenched him tightly as he thrust deeply inside her. The tips of his fangs scraped over her nipple and along the sides of her breast until she was one big bundle of quaking nerves, a time bomb set to go off at the slightest touch. She let her head roll back on the pillow to enjoy the ride.

Marco's thrusts grew quicker and more erratic. He was no longer gentle, his body ramming hers with force. She threaded her hands through his hair and pulled him closer for a kiss. The lingering taste of her blood in his mouth should have turned her off. It didn't.

It made her hotter instead. She was on fire. She was on the brink of what promised to be another earth-shattering climax, and all it would take was one stroke at just the right angle to do it. She shifted her hips a little and her world exploded. Marco came with her, his mouth leaving hers as a guttural cry escaped his lips.

He held his weight off of her, supporting himself on his elbows. She could feel him shaking above her and she tried to pull him on top of her. He resisted. He rolled to his back, bringing her with him and tucking her against his chest. His heart was pounding as hard as hers. He stroked her hair gently and brushed his knuckles across her cheek. "I'm sorry."

"For what?"

"I think I took too much." He sighed audibly. "I should have been more careful. I could have really hurt you this time."

"Don't be silly. I feel fine." But even as she said it, she felt a little light-headed. It was probably just his suggestion that did it. He hadn't fed for long.

"You won't later." He tucked a strand of her hair behind her ear and kissed the top of her head. "I'm not supposed to feel this way with you."

What was *that* supposed to mean? "Why not?"

He didn't answer. She looked up at him. His eyes were closed, but she knew he wasn't asleep. She decided not to ruin the afterglow and push it. She took a deep breath and let it out slowly before she settled against him. He wanted to stay tonight, fine. But in the morning he was going to have some talking to do. When they woke up and the euphoria was gone, she could interrogate him to her heart's content. For now, she'd back off. Who knows, maybe for once he'd decide to tell her something on his own, without her needling him first.

Chapter Nine

Marco was still sleeping when Amara woke up. Careful not to disturb him, she crawled out of bed, grabbed the robe she'd found hanging in the closet, and went down to the kitchen for breakfast. Or lunch, since it was nearing noon. Her whole schedule was disrupted, and she was beginning to wonder if she'd ever get back to where she'd been before she came here. Maybe she didn't even want to. She was kind of enjoying being lazy for once, instead of putting in fourteen-hour days on the set.

She looked through the cabinets, but nothing appealed to her. Giving up on the idea of food, she settled for brewing a pot of coffee, and, when it was finished, carried it into the living room. She'd been in the room before, but she hadn't really had a chance to study a couple of paintings that she'd noticed. She definitely wanted to get a closer look.

One in particular, an oil painting of an incredibly beautiful green valley, caught her attention. It was breathtaking. The ground was covered with trees, and a wide blue river cut through the bottom of the valley. A large white house sat near the top of the far hill, flanked by a rather large vineyard, but other than that there weren't many buildings around. She wondered where this was. It was a place she'd certainly like to visit someday, just to see if the view was as beautiful in person as it was on the canvas.

After a moment she knew Marco was behind her. She didn't need to turn to see, she just felt him there. It was a strange sensation, and a little unsettling. "Where is this place?"

If her newly acquired powers of perception bothered him, he didn't show it. He stepped closer and put his hands on her waist. "That's my home. It's the Douro River Valley in Portugal."

That explained the barely noticeable accent. "You're from Portugal."

"Originally, yes. That house was mine for a long time. I owned the vineyard for close to a hundred years."

"It's very beautiful." She was going to pretend the whole 'hundred years' part didn't bother her. "Why did you leave?"

"It was time to move on. I'd spent far too long mourning old ghosts, grieving a past that I could never get back. I sold the property and left." He nuzzled her hair with his chin. "The current owners have turned it into a bed and breakfast of sorts. Whenever I visit, I stay there."

"Do you visit often?"

"Not as often as I'd like, but I go when I can."

"I'd like to go with you sometime." It slipped out before she had a chance to stop it, and she wished she could take it back. He wouldn't keep her around long enough to be making trips to foreign countries with her.

He surprised her. "Would you really want to? I'd like that."

He seemed unusually receptive today, and she wanted to take advantage of it while she had the chance. "Tell me about your family."

He sighed. "My parents were farmers in the valley. They've been gone too many years. I had one sibling growing up, a brother."

"It must have been nice having someone to play with."

"We were close."

He was silent for a little too long. She was afraid that if she let him keep quiet much longer, he'd shut her out again. She wanted to know about him. "Do you work, or do you just go around kidnapping unsuspecting women?"

He laughed. "I've had many jobs over the years. I'm taking a break right now, but up until a few months ago I was a stock broker on Wall Street."

"You're kidding me." She had a hard time picturing Marco within a hundred feet of Wall Street.

"Nope. I did that for ten years. Now I think it's time for something else. I might go back to painting for a while."

"You paint?" She narrowed her eyes, trying to read the signature on the painting in front of them. "That's yours, isn't it?"

He nodded.

"Cardoso? So 'Just Marco' has a last name after all."

"That's the name I was born with, but I haven't used it publicly for a while." He shifted, pulling her back against him. "Is there anything else you'd like to know?"

It couldn't really be this easy. What was the catch? "How can you possibly afford to take time off? This house must have cost you a fortune."

"In four hundred years I've managed to accumulate enough to see to my needs." He paused and drew a deep breath. "I'm sure you can afford some time off, too."

"A little while, but I wasn't exactly careful about my spending habits." She hadn't expected to lose her job. Sometimes life bit the big one. "If you're still worried about me capitalizing on picking on your race, don't. Most of that money is gone." Some of it to Derek's drug habit and all the expensive rehabs, but she wasn't going to share that with Marco.

"I'm sorry." His voice was barely a whisper against her hair.

"For what? You didn't spend the money."

"Not about the money, Amara. About everything else."

It took her a moment to realize what he was saying. She pulled out of his arms and turned to face him. "If this is about kidnapping me, forget it. It's done. You can't take it back now. Let's just move on, okay."

Marco sighed and ran a hand down his face. He looked like he wanted to say something, but he didn't. He just stared at her, his expression a mix between guilt and pain.

She tried to lighten the mood. "Don't feel bad. I'm over it."

His expression darkened. When he spoke, his voice was a low growl. "You shouldn't be."

He stalked out of the room. She thought about going after him, but changed her mind. When he was ready to talk, and not growl, he knew where to find her. It wasn't like she was going to leave or anything.

*****

He was out of his mind.

Amara did *not* belong to him. She may have agreed to stay, for now, but that didn't give him the right to hold her to it. She'd been acting strangely for a little while—first the dizzy spell she had, and then her agreeable attitude. He hadn't known her long, but he knew enough to see that she wasn't putting up as much of a fight about staying as she normally would. Something with her wasn't right.

She'd never admit to it, though, so asking what was wrong would be pointless. She'd blame it all on stress, on the kidnapping, and the fact that she thought he was a lunatic.

She was right.

Somewhere along the line he'd plunged over the cliff of sanity. He just hoped it wasn't too late to redeem himself before she walked out on him for good.

He leaned back in his chair, propping his feet up on the desk he kept in the small study. The house was relatively quiet—he'd heard Amara sneak back upstairs after he left her. She was probably sound asleep by now, her curvy body splayed across his sheets. Her hair fanned across the pillow. *His* pillow.

He cursed himself for thinking such thoughts. He needed to stay away from her for a while and let the poor woman get some sleep. She could probably use a couple days' rest at the least. He'd been feeding too much. At this rate he'd drain her dry before he even got the chance to return her home.

That was another cause of conflict. His original intentions had gotten twisted along the way. Forget teaching the woman a lesson, he just wanted to find some way to keep her here short of strapping her to his bed for all eternity.

Not that strapping her to his bed wasn't an intriguing prospect. But, after the abduction from her home, he had a feeling she wouldn't go along with it, at least not yet.

This was confusing, to say the least. Never in his life had he imagined he'd ever be so infatuated with a woman he was so confused about. Now he just had to figure out what to do about it.

Chapter Ten

Amara sat in a chair facing the bay window in the living room, looking out into the quiet night. With the window cracked open to let in some of the cool spring air, the only sounds were crickets chirping and the occasional splash of the fish in the pond a few hundred yards from the house.

The moon was nearly full, and she was able to admire the serene beauty of the world around her. Why had she ever missed the city? She could get used to this. Too bad she'd never have the chance.

She'd been with Marco for a week. Pretty soon he'd get tired of her and send her home. That's what always happened—the men in her life got sick of her and moved on. Or, in Derek's case, slept with every man and woman on the west coast and just *neglected* to tell her.

It was a little past midnight, and she should be tired. But she wasn't. She was wide awake, even though she hadn't slept in almost a day. Marco had sent her to bed to get some sleep while he made a few phone calls, but she'd tossed and turned for two hours. Finally she'd given up. It wasn't worth the effort.

"What are you doing awake?"

She winced when he switched on the lamp next to the window.

"Hey, are you okay?" He sounded concerned.

She shrugged it off. "Yeah, I couldn't sleep."

She hadn't eaten all day, either, yet she wasn't hungry. She started to wonder if she was getting sick. It wasn't like her to not feel the effects of an empty stomach. She'd lived with starvation diets long enough to know the signs.

"Maybe you should see a doctor."

That would involve going back to the city. She wasn't ready. She'd gotten too used to Marco's quiet life, so far from the reality she knew, to want to go back. She shook her head.

"No?"

"No, Marco," she said. "I don't want to leave. Not to see a doctor, not for anything."

He looked worried, and a little upset. "People are probably starting to notice you're gone."

She shrugged. "Let them."

He placed a hand on each of her shoulders. "I have to take you back tomorrow, Amara."

"Tomorrow?" That couldn't be possible. She could not let that happen. "Why?"

"You don't belong to me. It's not right for me to keep you here like some kind of caged animal."

"What if I want to stay?" She didn't feel caged in any way. It had been a while since she'd felt threatened by him. Something had changed. She couldn't identify what it was, but it felt like everything in her universe had shifted when he'd knocked on her door. Being here, being anywhere, with Marco felt *right*. She knew she was asking for trouble by protesting, but she no longer cared. She wanted Marco, and she wasn't ready to leave just yet.

She was supposed to be here. She couldn't explain it to him, and he'd probably laugh it off if she tried, but she knew this was where she needed to be.

"You can't. Don't make this any harder than it is, sweetheart." He sighed. "I want you to see a doctor. This is really important to me. How about we compromise. You can see a doctor I know. He's going to come out to the house."

"What's the big push with the doctor? I've told you I'm fine."

He didn't speak for so long, she wondered if he was even listening to her. When he finally opened his mouth to speak, he sounded worried. "Look, there's something going on with you, whether or not you think you're fine. You aren't sleeping, you aren't eating, you're very pale and listless. I've seen this before. It could be the symptoms of..."

Her heart skipped a beat. "Symptoms of what?"

"Nothing. Never mind." He shook his head. "Just see the doctor, okay?"

She narrowed her eyes at him. "What part of this do you not understand? I don't want to see a doctor. I don't care whether he's a friend of yours or not."

He looked ready to protest, but a knock on the door stopped him. He opened the door and let in another big man. This one wasn't as dark and scary as Marco, though. With his long, dark blond hair pulled into a ponytail and the goofy tropical print shirt he wore, he reminded her of a typical, Southern California beach bum. He was imposing, but not in a way that scared her.

"What's this problem you wanted to talk to me about?" The stranger's gaze fell on Amara and he smiled knowingly. "I didn't realize you were keeping pets. Hey, you have a nice one here."

Marco winced. "It's not like that."

"Of course not. It never is." The man's gaze looked Amara over, very slowly, covering every inch of her body before it finally settled on her breasts. *Typical.* "Where did you find this one?"

She crossed her arms over her chest and tapped her foot on the floor. "First of all, my face is up here. Second, I'm not anybody's *pet.* I can make up my own mind, and make my own decisions. I'm here because I want to be, not because I'm being kept."

Well, everything but the last sentence was true, anyway, and that whole issue wasn't very clear anymore.

The man blinked and turned to Marco. "Since when did you go for the ones with minds of their own? I thought you liked them subservient and pliant."

He turned back to Amara. "Wait a minute, aren't you Midnight Morris?"

She sighed loudly. How many times in her life was she going to have to go through this speech? "*I'm* Amara Daniels. Midnight Morris is a fictional character who, according to Marco, should be tarred and feathered for getting every detail about the life of vampires so completely and utterly wrong."

He stared at her for several seconds before he burst out laughing. "Are you kidding? I love those movies."

"Royce." Marco's tone held a warning.

"What? Doesn't everybody?'

"Apparently not Marco." Amara rolled her eyes. "He thinks the writers could strive to make them a little more realistic."

Royce shrugged. "They could. It's not like we go around biting everyone or anything. But who cares? What's an immortal life if you can't have any fun?"

"Are you...?"

"A vampire? Yeah, I guess you could say that. I've got some really cool fangs, too. You want to see?"

Marco cleared his throat. "Once you've seen one set, you've seen them all."

"Oh, now that's not true. Mine are so much longer than yours."

Marco scoffed. "Size doesn't matter. Its how you use them that counts."

"Oh, yeah?" Royce winked at Amara. "Whoever coined that phrase was obviously pitifully small. Mine are huge, babe. That's what counts."

"As much as I hate to interrupt your fun, Royce, I called you for something a little more serious than a discussion of fang size." Marco shot Royce a dirty look, and Royce laughed.

"So what's the problem you mentioned on the phone?"

Marco shook his head. "We can talk about it later. When we have some time alone."

"You said we'd be alone tonight."

Marco shrugged. "I thought she'd be in bed."

She really hated it when people spoke about her like she wasn't in the room. Usually. This time, it might give her an advantage.

"She's not. So what?" Royce asked. "Is this something you'd rather she didn't hear?"

Marco sighed and shook his head. "Never mind. I guess it doesn't really matter."

Amara started to get out of the chair, intent on giving them some privacy, but that strange dizziness hit her again and she had to sit back down.

"Are you okay?" Marco asked.

She nodded, not able to speak. She took a couple of deep breaths. "I'm fine." Even to her own ears, her voice sounded weak. "I think if I just ate something, I'd be back to normal."

"Is *that* the problem?" Royce asked Marco.

Marco nodded tightly. "Yeah, she's been feeling a little…off lately."

Royce turned to Amara. "How so?"

"What does it matter to you?" she snarled.

"Just curious," he said. "No offense or anything, but you look like death warmed over."

Well, duh. She hadn't had access to her makeup bag in a week. "This is the way I look without all that stage makeup."

"No. You looked pale on screen, but that was probably on purpose. Now you look sick."

"I'm *fine*." What was it with the two of them? She could take care of herself.

Royce shook his head. "That's debatable. How are you sleeping?"

"*Fine*." She was starting to sound like a broken record.

"She's not," Marco chimed in. "At least not when she's supposed to."

"Are you eating?"

"She's not eating either. She's barely touched a meal in days."

Royce's expression was way beyond serious. "Hmm."

Okay, now she was getting genuinely worried. "Hmm? What's that supposed to mean?"

He ignored her, speaking to Marco instead. "Doesn't this situation strike you as a little odd?"

"Not really," Marco said defensively. "You heard her. She hasn't been eating well. That alone is enough to cause dizzy spells."

"I suppose." Royce turned back to her. "You're human, right?"

Her eyes widened in shock. "Of course."

"Both of your parents are human?"

"My mother is." Her mother was all too human. Her father—well, he could have been anyone. There had been so many men at the time her mother had gotten pregnant that she'd never been able to pinpoint exactly who'd fathered her child. But he was *human*!

Royce turned to Marco. "Did you feed off of her?"

Marco shrugged.

"I don't know how to explain this. Unless she's feeding off of you, too, this shouldn't be happening." Royce checked her pulse and frowned.

"What shouldn't? Somebody had better tell me what's going on really quick."

Royce looked her over for a full minute before he spoke. "If I didn't know any better, I'd swear…never mind."

"No, you have to tell me." After a statement like that, he wasn't going to blow her off. He'd better be planning on explaining himself.

"There's nothing wrong with her." Marco butt in. "She's been under a lot of stress lately." He really didn't want her to know the truth of what Royce was implying.

She grasped onto that thought, even though she knew something strange was going on in her body. She felt different, but couldn't explain how. She nodded along with Marco. "Yes, I'm fine. Nothing wrong at all."

"Yeah." Royce tilted the table lamp so the light was shining in her eyes.

She winced and covered her eyes with her hands. "What the hell did you do that for? Are you trying to blind me?"

"No. I'm trying to prove a point."

"What point is that? It's impossible to see when someone's shining a bright light in your eyes?" She glared at Marco. "If this guy's so inquisitive, I can just imagine what your doctor is going to be like."

Royce laughed at that. "I *am* the doctor."

"Oh, yeah right. And I'm the tooth fairy."

"He's a doctor, Amara. Has been for more years than you've been alive, and before that he was a healer." Marco answered.

"This is ridiculous. I'm fine. You just said the same thing. Why on earth did you feel the need to call a doctor?"

"I just wanted someone to reinforce that opinion," he said.

"You mean you wanted me to come in and lie to you," Royce said. "You wanted me to tell you all was great with her, when you already knew damned well that it wasn't. You know, for a smart guy you really can be stupid sometimes."

She started to ask more questions, but he shook his head again. She crossed her arms over her chest and leaned back in the chair. She'd just have to grill Marco later to find out what this guy was talking about. Doctor or not, he was wrong. She wasn't sick, just stressed. "Well, obviously you're not going to be of any help. Don't you have a practice to get back to or something?"

"He doesn't have a specific practice, he just goes where he's needed," Marco answered for Royce. "Once every couple hundred years he even visits me."

"That's not fair," Royce said. "It isn't my fault we didn't speak for so long."

"No. It isn't."

Marco was going all broody again. She wanted to ask about the story behind the cryptic comments, but now was probably not the best time to be asking questions.

Royce stared at her a little too long before he got up and walked over to where Marco was standing. "Why'd you let her do it? You knew damned well what could happen, and you let her do it anyway. You need to learn that you can't just *take* without thinking of the consequences."

"I didn't *let* her do anything. It was an accident, not something that was planned."

Accident? What accident? "Okay, this isn't funny anymore. Somebody had better start explaining, and quick."

They ignored her and continued their private conversation.

"That was pretty irresponsible, Marco."

"It was only a drop. Nothing's going to happen."

"A drop is all it takes." Royce ran a hand through his hair. "What are you going to do?"

"Nothing. There's no need to do anything, because *nothing* is going to happen."

"You're an idiot. It already has." He gave Marco a strange look before he left the room.

Marco walked over to her chair and knelt down in front of it. "How are you holding up? Think you can stand yet?"

At this point in time, she wasn't sure. "What's going on?"

He smoothed her hair away from her face. "Nothing. Royce gets a little overzealous sometimes. It's his nature."

"You've both got me a little worried."

"Don't be, sweetheart. Everything is going to be fine. Okay?"

She nodded, wondering exactly what was going on, and why no one would tell her anything.

* * * * *

Marco lay in bed as the sun rose, wondering what to do about Amara. He had to send her away, but he couldn't bear to do it. Something out here was affecting her in a bad way. He didn't know if it was being with him or the environment, but she was changing. She was starting to act like him, sleeping the same hours and refusing food.

Now he just had to convince Royce of that. Her problem wasn't as complex as Royce was making it seem. It couldn't be. As soon as Amara was returned home, she'd be back to her old self.

He wanted to keep her, but he would never do that to her. She might not care now, but she had a life to go back to, one he'd kept her from long enough. He would take her home first thing in the morning. She needed her life back more than he needed her.

And he *did* need her. There was just no way to keep her without turning her. If what Royce suspected was true, that wouldn't be an issue.

Royce was wrong. He had to be. Amara was just Amara. She would be fine once she got home. He'd made a stupid mistake in kidnapping her, but he really hadn't done anything else to endanger her.

"Marco?"

He hadn't realized she was there until she sat down on the edge of the mattress.

A jolt of guilt ran through him. He'd never once dreamed of ruining a life so completely. He'd made his share of mistakes, but this could quite possibly be his worst one yet. If he didn't let her go soon, bad things would happen.

"Go back to bed, Amara." He'd left her in his bedroom by herself and come to the guest room to get some sleep. Royce had left just before daybreak, but he'd promised to be in touch to see how Amara was doing. Between the two of them, they would have to keep an eye on her for the first couple of days she was back in her old life. He wouldn't let her get into trouble, even if he couldn't let her know he was there.

"I'll go, if you come with me."

"I can't do that."

"Then I'm staying right here."

He reached for her then. It was wrong for him to accept anything from her, on so many levels. He still hadn't explained to her what could be wrong with her. He wasn't ready yet to explain to her what Royce suspected. No need to worry her over something that might not even be true.

He couldn't accept it, not yet, but he couldn't totally deny the possibility, either. He just hoped everything would be okay. If he left her alone and stopped feeding from her, she might have a chance to recover.

If he hadn't taken so damned much of her blood to begin with, this might not even be an issue.

He held her for a long time, content to just lay with her on the narrow mattress. But she wasn't. She wriggled against him, her fingers stroking his chest. He hated himself at that moment. He could have ruined her life. He shouldn't have been so impulsive. If he'd just planned his actions, then he wouldn't have—

Amara kissed the side of his neck, sending a shiver through him. "Don't you want me anymore, Marco?"

He'd want her until the day he took his last breath. Considering his life span, that was saying a lot. "I don't want you to get hurt."

She sighed and settled back next to him. "You never did tell me how you turned vampire."

He froze, his senses on alert. Her growing curiosity bothered him, especially in light of what might be happening to her. "Why do you want to know?"

"How can I know how a real vampire lives if I don't know how one is created."

He said nothing, not willing to give her this, but not sure why.

She wouldn't let it go. "Does it really involve the exchange of blood?"

He sighed. "Yeah, I guess it does. But it's complicated, sweetheart. It's nothing you need to worry about."

It actually wasn't all that complicated at all. It would only take a little of his for the mutation to occur, especially if her blood was depleted from his repeated feedings, as it was now. He was in agony over how easy it would be to turn her. Then she would be his forever. He'd never have to let her go.

"Do it, Marco." Her voice was a whisper against his chest. "Make me yours."

He sat up on the edge of the bed, needing to distance himself from her before he did what she asked. It took a little while for him to realize that he hadn't spoken his desires out loud.

"How did you know what I was thinking?"

"I…I don't know. I just felt it."

"Is that really what you want?"

She came up behind him and wrapped her arms around him. She trailed her tongue along his neck, unerringly finding that place where she could break the skin and—

He had to remember she was not a vampire lover. The woman was human. If he allowed her to do this, her life would be altered forever. She might never forgive him, once she came to her senses.

But at the same time, he had to have her. Just one last time, and then it would be time to let her go. He needed this time with her, one more time to make love to a woman he'd come to realize he didn't hate at all.

Her teeth nipped at his neck like she'd been doing it all her life. He had to stop her. Flipping her onto her back, he pinned her body to the mattress. "What do you want, Amara?"

She smiled, a purely wicked smile that did more to arouse him than the touch of most of his lovers had been able to do. "Fuck me, Marco. Hard and fast. Just one more time before you make me leave."

He was more than happy to oblige. He tore at her clothes until she lay naked before him, sprawled on the bed like an offering. The thought that she would leave soon pushed him over the edge. He couldn't promise he'd be gentle tonight. He just hoped she didn't get hurt.

He tore at his own clothes and threw them in a pile on the floor. His cock ached at the sight of her pink lips, bared so completely to him. Would he be able to stay away from her for long? He didn't think so, but for her sake he'd have to try.

He stroked her labial lips softly with the tips of his fingers. She squirmed and moaned in protest, but he wasn't going to give her what she wanted just yet. He had his own memories to make. He thumbed her clit with long, slow strokes designed to drive her wild. He accomplished that easily—in a matter of seconds she was bucking against his hand.

"Come on, Marco. Please." She drove her hips against his hand, but he didn't give in to her demands.

"Relax. We have all day."

"I don't want to relax. I want to come!" She grabbed his wrist and tried to take control of his fingers, but he brushed her away.

She was acting the way he felt—like an animal, barely contained. It was killing him to keep control over himself, but he wanted today to last. If he let go and gave her what she wanted, he wouldn't last five seconds. At least this way, she'd get some attention, too. She deserved as much, since it seemed she'd finally accepted that their time together was coming to an end. Or was this just a ploy to make him let her stay? She'd been different in the past couple days, quieter, more accepting of everything. He had to wonder—what was she planning?

"Spread your legs for me, sweetheart." She narrowed her eyes, but obliged, moving her legs as far apart as she could. He skimmed his hands up the insides of her thighs before he bent down to give her an intimate kiss.

She cried out and rocked against him when his tongue touched her clit. He laved her thoroughly, bringing her to the brink of climax again and again before backing away. She whimpered and tore at the sheets every time he left her on the brink without giving her the release she begged for.

He finally delved his tongue deep inside her cunt, tasting her arousal and increasing his own. Stroking in and out of her was sheer madness. He was right on the edge himself, so much so that a gust of wind would topple him into orgasm. His cock ached, his balls burned, and he couldn't stand another second of waiting. One more flick of his tongue across her clit and she came, her juices pouring over his face.

"Sweetheart, you taste so good." He thrust his tongue into her again.

She moaned. "I want your cock, Marco, not your tongue."

He kissed his way up her body slowly, stopping to lave her distended nipples. Cupping her breasts in his hands, he suckled one nipple until she cried out again before pulling his mouth off and moving to the other. He'd never get enough of her taste. It drove him wild in a way he'd never experienced before.

She buried her hands in his hair and yanked his head up to meet hers. "Stop teasing me," she said through clenched teeth.

He laughed before he crushed her mouth with his in a kiss that left no doubt of his intentions. Teasing time was definitely over. Lifting her hips, he drove his cock into her cunt in one stroke. Amara moaned low in her throat, her body convulsing as he thrust hard and fast, making no apologies.

He'd never felt so out of control in his life. His fangs completely elongated against his will, something that hadn't happened in years. He tried to force them back in, but it was no use. Beyond the thinking stage, he sank them into her neck. Her blood flowed easily over his tongue and her nails dug into his back again. That was enough to send him into a furious climax that nearly blinded him. He buried his cock in her to the hilt and rode out the sensations, wondering if he was going to black out. He didn't, but he didn't have much strength left by the time he was done, either. A lot of that was probably due to the fact that he hadn't fed as often as usual since she'd been here. He hadn't wanted to leave the house to find a donor, but he couldn't feed off of her every time the need arose. Her fragile human body wouldn't be able to take it.

He didn't allow himself to feed for long. He pulled his mouth away, even though his thirst was nowhere near sated. Tomorrow he'd be able to get back to his regular schedule, feeding every night instead of every few, and feeding off of complete strangers. Without the emotional connection he felt with Amara, his senses wouldn't be so frazzled.

Amara pulled his head down for a kiss. Even after she'd just come, she was nearly crawling all over him. Her hands were everywhere. He knew she had to taste her blood on his tongue, but she didn't complain. In fact, she seemed to like it. She thrust her tongue into his mouth and moaned, her hand curling harder against his neck. He should have taken that as a sign to pull back, but he was too sated to read her actions.

He felt a quick stab of pain when she bit his lip. *Damn it.* She'd broken the skin again, and this was much more than a little nip. She'd gotten him good. He felt a line of blood trickle down the side of his chin. Before he knew what she was going, Amara licked his skin clean with one swipe of her tongue.

Floored, he pulled away. "What are you doing?"

She blinked, looking like Amara but acting like some kind of vampire vixen. "I thought you liked it rough."

He did, but he couldn't get rough with a human woman. "You bit me."

"You didn't seem to mind when I did it before."

"Yeah, well it's different now." That was an understatement. "What the hell is going on with you?"

"Nothing."

"You're scaring me. I'm supposed to be the unstable one."

She laughed at that. "You're not unstable. We all have our moments where we lose ourselves."

"Like you're having now?"

She shook her head. "No. I know exactly what I'm doing. I just can't stop myself. Maybe I don't want to."

She licked her lips, but there was nothing nervous about it this time. Another trickle of warm wetness trailed down his chin and he licked his own lip. He tasted the blood she'd drawn, *his blood*. And there was a lot more of it than last time, even more than he'd first thought. He shook his head. Good thing he'd pulled away, or else she might have—

There was no use even thinking about that. She hadn't gotten enough to do any permanent damage. Once he'd returned her home, she'd be fine. In a few weeks she'd be back to normal, sleeping at night and eating normal meals and *not* trying to drain him of his blood.

He hoped.

Chapter Eleven

This just sucked.

Two days ago Marco had brought her back to her townhouse, and he hadn't even bothered to call. *Not even once.* He'd promised her he'd be in touch, but that was a crock. She had hoped to hear from him, but she wasn't going to hold her breath. He'd gotten what he wanted from her, and now he was gone from her life.

How typical was that? Every man was the same when it came down to it. They took and took and took, and then they *left*. She didn't need him, anyway. She didn't need any man to make her life complete.

Never mind the fact that he'd had to drag her back home, literally kicking and screaming. Her neighbors probably thought she was out of her mind. First she was gone for days, then when she returned she acted like a total nutcase.

The thought of being separated from him had scared her to death. That was an odd reaction, considering how they'd met. But something inside her protested his choice to get rid of her. She didn't want that—she would have been perfectly happy to stay with him for the rest of her life. She'd assumed that once she'd been away from him for a little while she'd feel more like herself again.

She'd been wrong. She hadn't been able to stop thinking about him, trying to understand how he could wreak such emotional havoc on her in just a few weeks.

She'd never be the same, and being without him felt wrong.

Someone, probably the woman who'd brought her clothes when she was with Marco, had stocked her fridge and cleaned her house. Her car was right where she'd left it. Her mail was piled on the counter. It was as if nothing had changed, like she hadn't been gone at all.

Or it would have been, if her voicemail hadn't been littered with calls from Robby trying to get her to renegotiate her deal.

Ha! Like *that* would ever happen. But that didn't mean she couldn't have a little fun with him. She'd come to an important realization when she'd been with Marco. She didn't need that job. She didn't need Robby, or Derek, or Midnight. She was her own person, one who couldn't be threatened and pushed around, and it was about time Robby understood that.

She walked out into the bright sunshine of the afternoon and was practically blinded. Apparently all those days, and nights, in the woods were still affecting her. *Damn.* The sun had never bothered her before. She pulled her sunglasses out of her purse and put them on. *Much better.* Now she could at least walk down the sidewalk without falling over her feet.

When she got to the restaurant where she'd agreed to meet Robby, he was already sitting at one of the outdoor tables. He stood up when she approached, taking her hand in his and kissing it. She blinked. What the hell was that all about?

His smile was sickeningly sweet when he spoke. "Hey, baby. How are you doing?"

There was a nervousness about him she'd never noticed before. It made her laugh. To think that a few months ago, she'd considered getting down on her knees and begging this man for a job. She'd never actually seen him for what he was—a lemming so desperate to keep his job he'd jump through flaming hoops if the great powers-that -be told him to.

"Fine, Robby. How are you?"

He stared at her for a few seconds, his brow furrowed. "You look a little pale. A little too thin, too. What's going on with you?"

She shrugged and sat down. "Not much. I just took a much needed vacation."

"Usually you return my calls right away. I've been calling you for almost a week. That isn't like you, kiddo."

She hadn't done much of anything *like her* since she'd been back. There hadn't been time. Most of her days were still spent sleeping, although she was trying to break herself of the habit. Her nights were divided between late night movies and thoughts of Marco and why the hell hadn't he called…it had already been two days and he'd promised he'd be in touch—

The next time she saw him, he was in for a truck load of pain.

Robby was talking about something, but she couldn't focus on the conversation. The longer she sat outside, the more the noise bothered her. Too many people talking, too many car horns blaring. She couldn't stand it. How she'd ever lived in this city for so long was a mystery to her now.

"So what do you think?"

"What?" She looked over Robby's little, greasy-haired body and wished she was someplace else. Anywhere but here. Preferably anywhere she could be with a dark, sexy vampire. Naked.

"I was just telling you about the..."

She tuned Robby out again, concentrating instead on the dull throbbing that was starting in the back of her head. She needed a cup of coffee in a bad way, before it turned into a full-blown headache.

Robby's chattering wasn't helping. He went on and on, but she paid no attention to his words. She focused on the pounding in her head. Suddenly she had the oddest sensation of being able to *feel* the pulse beating in Robby's neck beating in time with the pounding in her head. She blinked and swallowed. Her throat had gone dry and her breathing had become ragged.

What the fuck was wrong with her? This was *Robby!*

"Amara, are you okay?"

She nodded and licked her lips, but it was a lie. She wasn't okay at all. She felt like she was going to pass out.

"Do you need me to call a doctor?"

"No." She needed that pulse...

"Are you on drugs or something?"

"What?" She had to struggle to understand what he said. "No, no drugs."

God, what she wouldn't give to just taste that vein—

Stop! Okay, she'd obviously spent *way* too much time living with a vampire. She shook her head hard and gestured for a waitress. She needed a cup of coffee.

Or maybe she needed vodka.

She needed something, and it sure as hell wasn't Robby's blood. She'd definitely been with Marco for a little too long. Now she was the one who was delusional.

Robby scooted his chair back a little while he spoke. "Um, the producers are willing to keep the movie softcore."

She laughed. "It's not going to happen, Robby. I don't need this job, and I don't need you."

She sipped the coffee the waitress set in front of her, but she gagged on the bitter taste. She added half a cup of milk, which helped a little. Even though it was cold, she could at least choke it down.

Shoving the cup away, she opted instead for the water the waitress brought with the coffee. At least that didn't have any flavor to begin with.

Robby blinked at her food choices. "Do you want something to eat, honey? You look like you could use it."

She shook her head and waved her hand in the air. "Not hungry. And just for the record, my name is Amara. If you call me honey, or baby, or anything demeaning like that again, I'm going to rip your throat out and stuff it up your ass. Okay?"

Robby's eyes widened and he scooted his chair back another couple of inches. When he spoke, his voice came out as a squeak, his head bobbing vigorously. "Yeah. Okay. Sorry. You really should eat something, though. You're wasting away."

She sighed. "You know, I really don't need you to run my life. This meeting was a bad idea. I'm going to leave before you make a fool of yourself by getting down on your knees and begging me in public."

"Is that what you want? You want me to beg?"

She had to admit, the idea held more than a little appeal.

"Why the sudden change?"

Robby looked at the ground. "Derek won't do the movies unless you do, too."

Of all the dirty tricks. "Derek can go fuck himself. I'm through with him."

"Come on, Amara. We need Derek. You've got to help me here."

"You need Derek? Why is it that everything is always about Derek? Are you screwing him, too?" She slammed her hand down on the table, making Robby jump.

He didn't answer, and he kept his gaze trained on the tabletop.

"I can't believe this. Why did it take me so long to see Derek for the asshole he is? Steve was bad enough, but *you*? What does your wife think about it?"

He sucked in a breath. "You can't say anything to Carol. Don't you dare."

"Please. It's not worth my time. *You're* not worth my time. If you need anything else from me, call my agent." She shoved her seat back and stood up. "On second thought, don't bother. He's fired. Goodbye, Robby."

She left him at the table, gaping and sputtering. Why had it taken so long to see what an idiot he was? She nearly laughed at the whole idea. Apparently Derek, the man who had claimed he would love her until her dying day, screwed anything that breathed within a ten-mile radius. The drug problems should have been a sign that there was something seriously wrong with him. If not the drugs, certainly his predilection for playing with dildos after they'd had sex should have tipped her off.

She'd let him walk all over her. She'd let everyone walk all over her, mainly because she was used to it. Her mother had done it, with her string of boyfriends and husbands, and when she'd struck out on her own she'd actually gone looking for it.

Her agent had bossed her around, and she hadn't thought twice. The directors she'd worked with had been the same. It was time she stopped that from happening. Now she just had to decide what she was going to do with the rest of her life.

She tugged at the collar of her shirt and wiped a couple beads of sweat off her forehead. Maybe she was coming down with something. It wasn't that hot outside, yet she felt like her blood was close to boiling.

Robby was right about one thing—she needed to eat. Food would make her feel better. Once she started eating like she used to—before she had to watch her weight and squeeze her body into clothing sized for a twelve year old boy—she'd feel better.

*****

She didn't have a chance to fix something to eat. A few minutes after she got home someone knocked on her door. A little wary, since the last time she'd had a visitor he'd kidnapped her, she opened the door a crack.

No angry blood suckers this time. It was a woman. "What can I do for you?"

"Amara? I thought we could talk for a while. I'm a friend of Marco's." The woman smiled. "My name is Ellie."

Sighing, Amara opened the door and let her in. She found it hard to believe that Ellie was only Marco's friend.

She was a good two inches taller than Amara, and supermodel thin. Her skin was so fair it appeared nearly translucent, and her shiny, black hair hung past her waist. Her eyes were a shocking shade of bright blue that stood out against her pale skin. The woman could make a fortune in Hollywood—the rail thin, pale look was hot right now.

A thought struck her. Even though Marco said she wasn't, Ellie looked like a vampire.

Ellie frowned. "Is something wrong?"

"You're not a vampire, are you?"

"No, I'm not." Ellie laughed. "I guess I'm just genetically cursed."

Amara snorted. Blessed was more like it. "So what is it you want to talk about?"

Ellie's expression grew serious. "Marco."

"Let me guess. You want me to stay away from him. I'm moving in on your territory, and you want me to back off."

Ellie's eyes widened in shock just before she burst out laughing. "Trust me. It's not like that at all. Marco is hardly my type. He's more of a brother to me than anything."

Relief washed over Amara. "That's good to know."

"Would it be possible to get a cup of tea?"

"Um, sure. I'll make a pot and we can sit in the kitchen to talk."

A few minutes later Amara swirled her spoon in her mug, knowing she wasn't going to be able to drink the tea. Just the smell alone killed her.

Ellie smiled sympathetically. "This is a tough time for you, huh?"

"You mean because that scumbag of a friend of yours dropped me off without so much as a goodbye and hasn't even bothered to call?"

"Actually, I meant..." She paused, her brow furrowed. "You know what...never mind. It's not important. So how does it feel to be back home?"

Was there some kind of a requirement that Marco's friends had to be so cryptic all the time? "It's fine, I guess. I just wish he'd call."

Ellie took a sip of her tea. "Would it make you feel any better if I told you he wants to?"

"No, it would make me feel better if he actually did." She shook her head. "Wanting to and following through are two very different things."

"He cares about you."

Amara shook her head. "He cared about getting what he wanted. He got it, and now he's moving on."

"That's not true. He cares a great deal more than he's willing to admit." Ellie sighed audibly. "He's a very stubborn man, and he can be a real ass sometimes."

Amara blinked at how easily that word slipped from Ellie's mouth. She looked so cultured, so collected. The cuss didn't fit her.

Ellie smiled, and Amara couldn't help but laugh. "Yeah, I have to agree with you on that."

Ellie was silent for a moment. She finished off her tea and set the cup down, leaning her elbows on the table. "You do care about him, don't you?"

Amara didn't even hesitate. "Of course I do." Probably a lot more than she should.

"He needs someone like you in his life, whether he realizes it yet or not. He's made some mistakes, and he's been hurt before, but I think you're good for him. Somehow I don't see you putting up with any of his crap." She patted Amara's hand. "Don't worry. He'll come around."

She shrugged. "We'll just have to wait and see. How did you two meet, anyway?"

"It was a long time ago. I feel like I've known him forever. I was, ah, having some problems with some neighbors and he stepped in."

"Enough said." She didn't want to hear the gory details. "Do you want another cup of tea?"

Ellie shook her head. "No, thanks. I have to go now, but I'll leave my number in case you ever want to talk again." She handed Amara a slip of paper. "Feel free to call anytime, if you need anything at all, okay?"

"I'm okay, but thanks."

She looked at the paper after Ellie left, surprised that Marco's number was there as well.

Chapter Twelve

"I am *not* calling him." Amara glared at the paper Ellie had left, now tacked to the bulletin board next to the fridge. "You shouldn't have bothered to give me his number, because there's no way in hell I'm picking up that phone."

She stirred the pasta on the stove, the whole time casting glances to the phone. *No.* She was not even going to think about picking it up. If he wanted to see her, he was going to have to make the first move.

Carrying the pan to the sink, she drained her dinner into the colander in the sink. The phone rang and she dropped the empty pan on the counter and ran for it, picking up the receiver on the second ring. "Marco?"

"Good evening, ma'am. This is Jeff calling from the—"

She slammed the phone back into its cradle. She didn't need to be bothered by telemarketers tonight. Grumbling, she turned her attention back to her meal.

"Stupid jerk. Would it really be that difficult to pick up the damned telephone and call me?" She took out her frustrations with Marco on the garlic and basil. By the time she was done, she'd turned them into mush.

Cursing, she added them to the sauté pan she'd heated the oil in. The second the seasonings hit the olive oil, she was hit with a wave of nausea so strong she had to lean against the counter. What was wrong with her? The smell of food cooking had never bothered her before.

Was she pregnant?

No. That wasn't possible. Those shots were very reliable, and she wasn't late. There had to be something else going on. But what was it, and how could she fix it so she could enjoy a decent meal?

After the sauce was ready, she mixed it with the pasta and brought a bowl of it to the table. She was going to eat the stuff, damnit, if she had to choke down every last bite. She'd been a little dizzy lately, and it was probably from not eating for so long. Once she had a couple of good meals in her, she'd be fine.

Ten minutes later she'd only been able to force down one bite, and that had been more than enough. This used to be her favorite recipe. Now she couldn't deal with the pungent flavor. Just the smell of it made her gag. How was she supposed to force down the entire bowl when it made her want to throw up?

"I'm glad to see you're eating." Marco's voice came out of nowhere. He hadn't been there a moment before.

She screamed and dropped her fork, sauce splattering all over the table and her clothes. Her eyes narrowed when she realized who had spoken. Jumping up and turning to face him, she put her hands on her hips. "How dare you sneak in here like everything is all right? I haven't seen you for days. What gives you the right to just show up without calling or anything? Haven't you ever heard of etiquette? The polite way to visit someone is *not* to sneak up on them while they're eating without bothering to pick up the phone and call first!"

He said nothing. He just stood in the kitchen door, his big shoulder propped against the doorframe. His expression was serious. A little too serious. It made her nervous. She bit her lower lip and waited.

"I couldn't stay away." His confession froze her, the tantrum gone. "I tried, Amara, honest to God I did. But I couldn't stop thinking about you."

"You could have *called*." She was beginning to sound like a broken record. Tears welled in her eyes and she swiped at them, not willing to admit that a *man* could get the new and improved Amara Daniels worked up.

"I've already done enough damage. I didn't want to hurt you any more."

"You hurt me by staying away."

"Don't you think I know that?" A look of genuine pain crossed his face. "It practically killed me to stay away, but there was nothing I could do."

She smiled weakly. "Do you want some dinner?"

He shook his head.

"You really don't eat, huh?"

"Not *that*. My needs are different."

Didn't she know it. "Yeah, I'm beginning to think the same thing myself."

"You still haven't been eating well?"

She shook her head. "No. I haven't been hungry. It's probably all the stress."

The silence that stretched between them was more than uncomfortable, but she didn't know what else to say to him. Marco finally broke the uneasy quiet. "I guess I did put you through a lot of unnecessary stress."

She shrugged. "It's no big deal. I survived." She tried to smile to show him she was fine, but it was becoming harder and harder by the second. At this rate, she'd be bawling at his feet in no time.

He shook his head. "I almost didn't."

She couldn't stop the tears now. They streaked down her face, probably taking most of her mascara with them. If they didn't resolve this quickly, she was going to end up looking like a raccoon.

He didn't move, but she could swear she felt him closer. The heat of his body moved over her, enveloping her like he was just a few inches away. She closed her eyes and greedily absorbed his heat. He'd deprived her of it for so long it hurt.

Wait a second, hadn't it only been a couple of days?

It felt like an eternity. It no longer mattered that she should hate him for not calling, not to mention scaring her with his sudden appearance. She could torture him later. Now she just wanted him to hold her. "What are you doing standing all the way over there?"

He dismissed her question with a shake of his head. "I didn't want to hurt you, Amara. I swear, I never meant to."

"The only thing that hurt me was when you deserted me."

He crossed the room in three steps and she was in his arms. Just like that she melted into him. He kissed her, deeply and desperately, and she knew she wasn't the only one who'd been feeling deprived. She moaned into his mouth and clung to him, afraid he'd walk away again. The man was like an addiction—one she'd never be able to break. Only when she was with him did she feel whole.

When did she turn into such a sap?

He broke the kiss, but didn't let her go. His arms were wrapped so tightly around her she had trouble breathing. "Hey, could you loosen up a bit before I pass out?"

He laughed once and loosened his grip a little. "How's that?"

"Better. I've missed you so much."

"It's only been a few days."

A few days when she'd lived in her own personal hell, not sure where she belonged anymore. "Tell me you haven't felt the same."

"This is too strong. I can't control it." He closed his eyes briefly. When he opened them again, she saw worry and raw desire in his gaze. "God, Amara. I've tried. I've tried to stay away from you, but I can't make myself do it."

She ran her nails along the line of his jaw, eliciting a shiver from him. "Why bother trying?"

Chapter Thirteen

"I know there's a reason why I should walk away, but I can't remember what it is." He pushed her shirt up and ran his hands over her bare waist before he pulled the shirt over her head and tossed it aside. "Maybe you should refresh my memory."

And give him a reason to walk back out of her life again? He had to be kidding. "Instead of concentrating on the reasons you should leave, why don't we concentrate on the reasons why you should stay?"

He cupped her breasts in his palms and bent down to suckle her nipples through her bra. The combination of his hot mouth and the scratchy lace made her knees buckle. His tongue moved over the puckered nipples, soaking the fabric.

"And what would those reasons be?"

Thinking of anything at all was becoming a challenge. "That there's something good going on here, and it would be stupid to waste it just because we met in such an unorthodox manner?"

He looked up at her and shook his head. "I guess I got lucky with you. Any other woman would have run screaming to the police the second I set her free. Why is it that you didn't?"

"Because I know you didn't mean me any harm, at least not after the first day or so. And I think you would have let me go if I'd protested enough."

He blew out a breath. "You're right. As much as I've tried to convince myself otherwise, I never intended to hurt you."

"Does that mean you actually care about me?"

"Don't push it, Amara." He shook his head, but his eyes told her all she needed to know.

His fingers skimmed up her back, unclasping her bra and sliding it off her shoulders. She shivered when his mouth met her bare breasts. He flicked his tongue across the sensitized flesh, using his lips to pull and pluck her until her panties were drenched.

She tunneled her hands in his hair and held him close while he suckled first one nipple, and then the other. She cried out when his fangs gently nipped her breasts. "I don't think I can stand up much longer."

He didn't answer. He nudged her legs apart and slid his knee between them, his thigh brushing against her aching clit. Suddenly she became all too aware that they were both overdressed for the occasion. She tugged on his shirt, but couldn't get her shaking fingers to work right. "Will you get out of these clothes?"

"Soon." He ran his tongue along her neck as he unbuttoned her jeans. "Very soon."

He pushed her jeans down her hips and she stepped out of them. Then his leg was back between hers, his thigh moving back and forth along her clit only separated by the thin lace of her panties. She rocked against him shamelessly, needing release.

He wouldn't let her have it. Just when she thought one more second and she'd come, he moved his leg and stepped away from her. Her legs were weak and wobbly and she almost fell. He brought his hands to her hips and held her up while he knelt down in front of her.

"What are you doing?" If he had in mind what she thought he did, there was no way her legs were going to hold her.

"Trust me."

"I do trust you. It's me that I'm worried about. I can barely stand as it is."

He nuzzled his nose against her mound through her panties. When he traced her labial lips through the lace with the tip of his tongue she almost died. He slipped a finger into the elastic leg band and followed the same path his tongue had before he ripped the panties from her body.

She gasped as the cool air hit her skin. Goosebumps broke out on her flesh, but they didn't last for long. He spread her lips with his thumbs and stroked her clit with the rough pad of his tongue. Forget chilled—she was burning up.

She arched her back and leaned into the counter behind her. He delved his tongue into her cunt, thrusting in and out a few times before he returned his attention to her clit. He took the bundle of nerves into his mouth and sucked hard. That was all it took for her to come, screaming and bucking against him. Every muscle in her body clenched and she couldn't take any more.

He didn't stop, though. He continued to suck and lick her, stroking his tongue inside her until she came two more times. By the time he stood up and pulled her into his arms, she wouldn't have been able to stand on her own if she'd wanted to.

Amazingly, the feeling of Marco's rock-solid cock pressing against her through his jeans ignited another wave of hot desire. She fumbled to unzip his pants, needing him inside her.

She finally freed his straining cock and wrapped her hand around the length of him. She stroked him a few times before she ran her fingers over the head.

Marco groaned, long and low, and thrust against her hand. "That feels so good."

"That's the point."

"You've got to stop."

She stilled her hand. "Why stop if it feels good?"

"Where's your bedroom?"

"Upstairs, first door on the right."

She smiled to herself when Marco picked her up and carried her all the way there. No man had ever bothered to do that for her before. The fact that she really wasn't a lightweight made it even more romantic.

He laid her down on the bed and stripped off his clothes before he joined her. He tried to roll her onto her back, but she wasn't going to let him take charge just yet. She smiled to herself, thinking she owed him a little for the days he hadn't bothered to acknowledge the fact that she was alive.

She put her hand on his chest. "Lay down."

"This is no time for games. I can't hold out much longer."

"Oh, I think you'll be surprised." She gave his shoulders a shove. "Lay down."

He started to protest, but then changed his mind and reclined on the mattress. His gaze was wary—she intended to change that. He wasn't used to women taking charge, at least not in the bedroom. She was going to change that, too. She was having too much fun to quit.

Plus, she wanted him to get used to letting her take charge. She could go for a little submission once in a while, but only if it was give and take in equal portions. Marco had already had his turn being in charge, and she was going to relish every second of her time.

She stretched his arms over his head and pressed his wrists to the pillows. "Keep them there."

He shook his head. "No way. I want to touch you."

"No touching. Not yet."

"That's not fair." He started to lift his arms.

She raised an eyebrow. "Oh, and kidnapping me was a fair thing to do?"

He let his arms drop back to the pillows with a dramatic sigh. "You've got a point there. Just be gentle."

Gentle? She had no intentions of that at all.

She ran her hands up his sides, scraping her nails along his skin with enough pressure to leave a red mark. He hissed out a breath and let his head roll back against the pillow. The struggle to do as she asked was plain in his eyes. It was killing him, but at least he was trying. She didn't know how much longer he'd hold out before he took her control away and took the lead.

She leaned over him and trailed a line of kisses across his chest. She licked his nipples and dipped her tongue into his navel, wanting to taste every inch of his exposed flesh.

Especially his jutting cock.

She didn't have much experience in pleasuring a man orally. It wasn't something that had interested her before, so she'd avoided it on most occasions. But for him she was more than willing to make an exception. She wanted to taste him. Just the thought of holding his throbbing shaft between her lips made her mouth water and her cunt quiver.

She darted her tongue out to wet her suddenly dry lips and Marco groaned. Her eyes widened when she saw the mixture of pain and heat in his eyes.

"Suck me, Amara. I need to feel your mouth on my cock."

She ran her tongue up his length experimentally. He was so soft, yet steely hard at the same time. She swirled her tongue over the plum-shaped head and he thrust his hips at her. Confidence bolstered, she licked the drop of pre-cum from the tiny opening. She closed her eyes and sighed indulgently. "You taste incredible."

Marco's resulting groan was harsh. She ducked her head to hide the laughter that bubbled up inside her.

Cupping his balls in one hand, she traced their skin lightly with the fingernails of her other. He hissed and started to lift his arms again, but she shook her head. "Stay where you are or I'm going to have to be forced to hurt you."

"God, Amara. Just do it. I can't take any more of this."

She took him inside her mouth, stroking up and down. She was just getting into a good rhythm when he pulled her off.

She sputtered in protest. "Hey. I told you not to touch."

"I had no choice. I was going to come."

She wouldn't have minded, but apparently he had other things in mind. He got behind her and pushed her belly onto the mattress, covering her body with his. He kissed her neck just before he bit down, his fangs sinking deep inside her flesh.

She screamed, nearly ready to come just from the pain and pleasure of it. It seemed that every time he did that, the pleasure got more intense. It didn't last long enough this time. Almost as soon as he started, he pulled back.

She was about to protest when he pulled her hips up into the air, leaving her upper body on the bed. She felt more open, more exposed than she'd ever felt in her life, but she didn't feel vulnerable. She felt safe with him, no matter what he did to her.

He dipped his fingers into her soaked cunt and ran them along her labial lips, spreading the moisture all over her. He pressed the tip of his cock against her, rubbing it across her clit. Every nerve in her body jumped.

"You teased me." His tone was accusatory, but not menacing.

"I did." She moaned softly as he continued to rub his cock along her folds. "And I think you enjoyed every second of it."

He laughed. "Yeah, probably a little too much. Another few strokes of that amazing tongue of yours and I would have come all over your face."

That thought sent a rush of pleasure through her body. "Next time, you will."

He pushed his cock into her cunt, filling her completely in one stroke. He didn't even pause. His strokes were hard and irregular, his balls smacking against her flesh. She fisted the sheets in her hands and held on tight, poised on the verge of another incredible orgasm.

Something inside her was different this time. She felt like she had that last time they'd been together, when she'd been so frenzied and wild. It was like something deep inside her was taking over, a part of her that she had no control over. Her entire body tingled—she felt aroused right down to the tips of her toes.

She was having trouble drawing a full breath. She needed...something, but she couldn't figure out what it was. She was on fire, but she didn't know what it would take to put the fire out. Marco's fingers brushing her clit was all it took to topple her over the edge. She came with a moan, clenching her inner muscles tightly on his cock.

His erratic breathing turned into a drawn-out groan as he stilled and came, emptying himself inside her. When he pulled out and let her go, she collapsed on the bed, too sated and boneless to move. He reclined beside her, drawing small circles on her back with his fingertips.

It was a long time before she was even able to form a complete thought, let alone talk. When she finally spoke, she had to keep it simple. "That was so..."

"Yeah. I know what you mean."

"Are you okay?" She raised her head a little to look at him but found it was too much effort. She flopped back down against the soft pillow and sighed.

He laughed. "I don't know. Are you?"

"Yes." She was okay, but that odd sensation hadn't gone away. It had lessened with orgasm, but it hadn't gone away. It was a dull throb low in her belly, a little like desire but not quite. She would have said it was similar to what she'd felt at lunch that afternoon when she'd thought about Robby's blood, but it was too creepy to connect what she had with Marco to anything about Robby.

Still, the feeling was there and it wasn't going away.

"Amara?"

"Mmm." Talking was still an effort.

"We need to talk."

His sentence broke through her sensual fog. "What's the matter?"

"There's something I need to tell you. It's not exactly good news."

Chapter Fourteen

She reared up on the bed, ready to strangle him. "You're not gay, are you?"

He laughed, but his expression was disbelief warring with horror. "Are you nuts? After what just happened, how can you have any doubts?"

"Okay, sorry. I just seem to have a problem with that lately."

He sighed. "I'm not your ex."

No, he most certainly was not. "What is it you want to talk about?" If he wasn't gay—which was a very good thing—what could the problem possibly be? "You're leaving me, aren't you?"

"No." He looked just a hair beyond irritated. "Will you just listen to me for a minute?" She nodded. He took a deep breath before he continued. "You haven't been feeling any better, have you?"

She wanted to deny it, to tell him she was feeling like her old self, but it wasn't true. She couldn't lie to him when he was staring at her with such a concerned expression.

"I'm feeling…actually, I'm feeling worse."

"This shouldn't be happening. Damn it. Why did I let this happen?"

"You sound like Royce. Are you going to explain to me what the problem is?"

He sat up in bed, leaning against the headboard. "It's a really long, complicated explanation."

She blinked. "An explanation you owe me, complicated or not."

"Okay, I'll try my best. What I told you before about blood sharing wasn't completely true. A vampire is someone with a genetic mutation in their blood. It's not sharing blood that causes it. It isn't a disease, exactly, but I guess in a way it is."

"What the hell are you trying to say? You've got me more confused than ever."

He shook his head. "Just listen. I'm trying to tell you something here. Blood doesn't need to be exchanged. A lot of times that's what happens, but it's not necessary. If a human's blood is infected with blood that contains the mutated gene, they can become a vampire."

"It's an infection?"

"I suppose you could look at it that way. But it's not one that can be cured."

"And you're telling me this *why*?"

"You asked me before for an explanation."

She had. But now she wasn't so certain she wanted to know. "Let me see if I've got this right. A human can become a vampire if their blood is exposed to vampire blood. So it's like a blood-born pathogen?"

He nodded. "Exactly."

Her blood chilled when she realized where he was going with this. It wasn't an innocent explanation at all. She licked her lips. "How easy is it for someone's blood to become infected?"

He spoke carefully, very slowly. "It depends on the amount of blood and the condition of the human's immune system. With a drop of blood the chances of the mutation occurring are pretty slim."

"But it's possible."

He let out a breath. "Yeah. It's possible."

"This is about when I bit your lip."

He nodded.

"You don't think...that I'm…"

He nodded again, very slowly. He reached out to touch her, but she scooted away, shaking her head. "You're wrong. I'm fine. I would know if my blood was *mutating*, wouldn't I?"

"Don't you?"

She said nothing. She didn't know what to say. What he was telling her wasn't possible. It just couldn't happen to her. This had to be another bad dream. No, not a bad dream. A nightmare.

"There's got to be something we can do to return me to normal."

"It's not like there's a medication for it or anything. Once you're infected, it's for life."

She shook her head, hoping somehow what he was saying would go away. "No. There's got to be a way."

"There is. Learn to live with it."

She looked at him, still shaking her head around like some stupid bobble head doll. "I'm still human, right?"

"You'll have to use that description loosely from now on."

Okay, this was *so* a nightmare. "If I wait out whatever it is, will it go away?"

"You don't get it. It isn't a virus, it's a genetic mutation."

"So now I'm…"

"Consider yourself mutated."

"No. I don't want this. All I want is my old life back." Or her lack thereof, as the case was. She wanted to go back to being a nice, semi-normal, unemployed girl. This was nuts. "What can I do to make it go away?"

"There's more." He reached for her, but she swatted at his hands.

"You did *not* just tell me that I'm a vampire, and you're *not* going to give me any more bad news tonight." She put her hands over her ears and started to hum.

"Amara?"

"I'm sorry. I can't hear you!"

He lifted her hands off her ears and her humming stopped. She blinked a few times, fat tears welling in her eyes for the second time tonight. This wasn't like her. She *never* cried.

Well, it wasn't exactly an everyday occurrence that her lover informed her she'd accidentally turned herself into a vampire.

"It's going to be okay."

Her hopes soared with that statement. Next he was going to tell her this was all some big, twisted joke. She was fine, just majorly stressed out. No mutated blood in this girl.

"You're going to have to feed before you get sick."

And then those hopes crashed to the ground. Not only crashed, but crashed and burned.

Crashed and burned, taking down the entire city of Los Angeles with them.

"I have to *what?*" Her voice escalated and she felt like throwing up or crying. Or maybe hitting something really hard.

Like Marco's face.

"The mutation takes a long time to happen. It can take days, or even weeks, but once it's complete, you'll die if you don't feed."

"It was only a drop! I didn't know this would happen."

"I never should have touched you." He snorted. "If I'd known what you were going to do, I would have stopped you."

She didn't doubt that. It was her own dumb fault for wanting to force him to let go and be himself with her. She shook her head. "It isn't your fault, you know."

He snorted. "Well, yeah, it is. If I'd just left you alone, then none of this ever would have happened."

She blew out a breath. "I don't even know what to say to you."

"You're in agony."

Well, she wouldn't exactly describe it as agony, but it wasn't a day at the park either.

"I can help you with that."

"How?" She was almost afraid to ask.

"By helping you feed."

"Oh, no. I'm not going to have you bringing strangers into the house so I can suck on their necks."

This time he actually laughed. "I wouldn't want you drinking from some stranger. I meant me."

"Really?" She blinked. "I could do that?"

His smile was purely wicked. "I would love you to do it. I've wanted that for a long time."

She swallowed hard. "Um, I don't know. Will it help?"

"Well, it couldn't hurt. Besides, you need to eat. At this rate you're going to waste away before you've had a chance to get used to this."

She could see from the look on his face that he didn't want that to happen. Dammit, neither did she. Whatever happened to her, however much this vampire and living on blood crap affected her life, she wasn't ready to *die.*

She couldn't forget the fascination she'd had with Marco's blood. Now she understood why. She hadn't been going crazy, she'd been turning into a mutant freak.

It didn't matter, not when she could practically feel that hot blood pounding in his veins. She wanted that blood. She wanted to taste it, let it flow into her mouth…

Licking her lips, she realized it was becoming something of a need. Her pulse kicked up a couple of notches and she was surprised that she was becoming sexually aroused even though she'd just been sated more times than she could count.

"Tell me something, Marco. Does your kind always feed off each other when they make love?"

He shrugged, but something sparked in his eyes. "It's common practice."

"How do you handle it? I got so dizzy."

"It will be different. I promise."

"I don't want to hurt you."

He laughed. "Please, hurt me."

She ran her tongue over her teeth. Her nice, normal humanoid teeth. "How am I supposed to…?"

"It will be okay. Trust me on this."

* * * * *

Marco waited for an eternity, watching every emotion from desire to fear to denial and indecision war in Amara's eyes. His cock was already hard with anticipation of what she was about to do.

Or what he *hoped* she was about to do.

She was afraid, and he understood that fear. His own turning had been very different, because he'd been bleeding out at the time. With not much of his own blood left in his body, the mutation had taken effect almost immediately.

And he'd *wanted* it. He'd practically begged for it. He'd been dying. Amara was young and full of life. She still didn't understand that this life could be the most amazing thing that had ever happened to her.

He had another reason for asking her to feed off of him. It would increase the bond between them that he knew was already stronger than it should be. When she'd left, it had been torture. This was a way to bind them for life, so he wouldn't be able to push her away again.

He snorted. Now there was no reason to push her away. He didn't have to fear losing control and turning her without her permission. Her ingestion of his blood had been a terrible accident, but something good had come out of it. He would have his woman for life.

He just hoped she'd be as understanding when she'd had time to let the enormity of the situation sink in. She might be fine with all of this now, but tomorrow or the next day, when she finally understood what she now was, she would probably have a few choice words for him.

That was why he fully intended to make the most out of tonight. If he could show her just how incredible her life could be, maybe she wouldn't turn away from him when she finally understood what he'd done to her.

"Come here, Amara."

He half expected her to turn away from him, but she didn't. She crawled across the bed and straddled his lap. That was all it took to drive him completely mad. He fought the urge to thrust against her, thrust *into* her. Whatever she needed, he'd have to let her take it on her own.

"I want you, Marco." Her voice was barely above a whisper, but it sent shivers through his body. He'd been waiting for a woman like her all his life. Considering the length of his life that was saying a lot.

He decided to lighten the moment when he saw the abject fear in her eyes.

"Do with me what you will, woman." He let his head drop back, offering his neck to her in mock-surrender. "I am yours for the taking."

She laughed. He loved the sound of her laughter.

"Do you know how beautiful you look tonight?"

She raised an eyebrow. "You're a little biased."

It was his turn to laugh. She didn't know how right she was. Even before he'd taken her, he'd seen what an incredible beauty she was. It wasn't that she was stunning. Her features were more interesting than classically beautiful. Her beauty had a lot more to do with the chemistry between them, and quite a bit to do with the fact that she was the first woman in four hundred years who'd challenged him regularly and still turned him on.

He lifted his head a little. "What are you waiting for? Don't leave me hanging over here."

Her laugh this time was pure sin. She wrapped her hand around his cock and stroked him a few times. "It feels like you're hanging pretty well to me."

If she didn't feed soon, he was going to flip her onto her back and fuck her. Then they wouldn't get around to her feeding for a while, and he didn't want to prolong it any longer. He wanted to give her a chance to find out what a rush feeding was. It might help her accept it better later on. But if she didn't hurry up and—

His thoughts ended abruptly when she took his cock in her mouth. He moaned and thrust into her mouth, too far gone for anything else. At the last second he snapped back to his senses. He had to stop her before this really got out of hand. That first time was difficult, but with any luck he'd have her feeding regularly in no time. Lifting her by her shoulders, he pulled her up and against him.

Her drenched labial lips pressed firmly against his cock and her hardened nipples were flush against his chest. He wasn't going to last another second. "I need this from you, Amara. I do."

With a hand on the back of her head, he guided her toward his throat. At first she just ran her tongue along the skin, driving him to the brink of madness. Then her teeth nipped. It wasn't hard enough to break the skin, but his cock twitched against her. He couldn't help it. He moaned, more from the anticipation than the actual sensations.

He'd only turned a human one time in his life, and the disastrous results of it was something he would rather forget, if only he could. Most of his knowledge of the subject came from Royce, who'd done a lot more studying on the subject. So, in a way, this was a new experience for both of them.

He expected a great deal of pain from her dull human teeth. He was surprised when the sting he felt was sharp but momentary. She was a lot further turned than he'd expected. Her blood must have been infected immediately. He'd have to keep her away from mirrors. If she saw the fangs he knew she now possessed, she'd go into shock.

The first lap of her tongue was tentative. Soon she grew bolder. Eventually she latched on and suckled him hard. He couldn't take another second of this. Lifting her hips, he thrust his cock into her cunt. She gasped against him, but soon was riding him with abandon.

She cried out, her orgasm taking her by force. She bucked against him, her mouth sliding away from his neck. He pulled her in for a kiss, cleaning away the trickle of blood at the corner of her mouth with his tongue. Tasting himself on her only increased his pleasure.

Whether she knew it or not, Amara now belonged to him. *Forever*.

If she'd have him. They still had a lot of talking to do, and she had a lot of his transgressions to forgive. They knew each other in the physical sense, but if he thought about it, he didn't really know her as well as he wanted to.

He planned to change that. Soon. But for now, he'd be content with what she'd give him. If that were only physical, he'd accept that on a temporary basis.

The last thought was gone as his own orgasm took him. His thoughts shattered as he spurted himself inside her. Inside his woman. *His* woman. He never thought that phrase would enter his mind again, but it had snuck up on him when he'd least expected it.

If he had to admit it, he even kind of liked the sound of it.

Amara flopped back on the mattress, spreading her arms. "Wow."

He couldn't help the smugness he felt at her comment. "You think?"

"Oh, please. I know you felt it, too."

"How do you know that?"

He settled in next to her, rubbing his hand up and down her thigh.

"This is going to sound strange, but I *felt* how you did when you came. I, um, could feel what you were feeling pretty much the whole time." She furrowed her brow. "Then again, it probably doesn't sound all that strange to you, does it?"

Strange didn't even begin to describe it. As far as he knew, the only vampires who could read minds were the ones who were psychic as humans. He shrugged. What did he know? He'd spent the better part of four hundred years emotionally ignoring just about every vampire he'd met.

"In all honesty, this is pretty new to me, too."

"How?"

"I've never let myself get attached before." Mentally, he'd preferred to keep his distance. He hadn't been able to do that with Amara, not from the start.

"Are you attached now?"

"You'd better believe it."

He wasn't about to tell her how cute she looked with her budding fangs.

She blinked hard and ran her tongue along her teeth. "My what? Oh, God. I can't believe this."

He just stared at her, not knowing what to think. He hadn't spoken that thought out loud.

Her brow furrowed even further. "I thought you said vampires can't read minds."

He shook his head. "No. I said *I* can't read minds. Some can, others can't. It really depends on what they were as humans." Then what she was saying hit him. "Are you telling me you read my mind?"

She nodded slowly. "I guess. It was more of sensing your thoughts than an actual reading. It wasn't very in-depth, just a touch."

"You sound like you know what you're talking about."

"Yeah. My grandmother was a fortune-teller in one of those little shops back home. It was one of those tourist attraction things." She rolled her eyes. "She did it for years. From what I'm told, she made some pretty good guesses, too."

A mental light bulb went on in his mind. "Your grandmother was a psychic?"

Amara laughed. "No, silly. She was a palm reader at a campy little fortune telling shop. That's all a bunch of bunk, anyway."

"Like vampires?"

Her eyes widened. "Oh…my…God."

He sighed. If she'd inherited even a small amount of psychic abilities, she was going to be one powerful vampire.

Chapter Fifteen

She'd fallen asleep sometime in the midst of their discussion. When she woke up, her mouth felt like she'd been sucking cotton and her head throbbed. But she didn't feel hungry anymore.

Creepy.

She found Marco sitting at the kitchen table, reading the newspaper. Such a normal thing to do, for a man who was anything but. Her own emotions were in turmoil.

She tapped her fingernails on the table to get his attention. "So what happens now?"

She waited for him to tell her last night had been a dream. She was most certainly not about to become a vampire.

She couldn't, seeing as vampires didn't exist.

Marco was just a crazy fan who, even though he was sexy as hell and up for anything, needed some serious medication.

She could ignore the fangs, she could ignore the whole drinking blood thing—hey, everyone was different—but she couldn't ignore the fact that he'd kidnapped her and locked her in a room when it should have been he who was locked away...hell, this wasn't working. She felt different, she had *fangs*, and she didn't like it.

He smiled and winked. "What do you want?"

A million dollars, a new house, a lover who *didn't suck blood…* "You know what I mean."

"I don't think I do." He sighed and ran a hand through his hair, obviously trying his hardest not to look upset. "Are you okay with all of this?"

Okay? *Okay?* Not only did she find out her grandmother was probably not a fraud, making her have some kind of strange, out-of-this-world powers, she was also turning into a total freak of nature. What kind of a life was that?

She stomped around the room, trying to decide if she should yell at him, or cry. Technically, it wasn't all Marco's fault. She'd bit his lip. But he should have told her what could happen. If he had, she never, *never*, would have considered doing anything to him that might break the skin.

Right?

Her hands were shaking. In fact her whole body was shaking. She hated Marco, hated herself for doing that. Why had she even let him in the same bed with her in the first place? She should have kicked him out, delusional bastard that he was. She had enough stress in her life right now. She didn't need this, too.

"I want you to leave." She struggled to keep her fury under control.

He shook his head. "Nope. Sorry. Anything but that. I'm not leaving you alone right now. It isn't safe."

"Why the fuck not?" She tried to keep her voice down, but it was no use.

Marco looked shocked. "Listen. I know this can be a pretty scary thing. I don't want you to have to go through it alone."

She glared at him. "I *like* being alone. I crave aloneness, oneness with myself and the environment. Besides, you left me alone for days."

"That's beside the point. A couple hours ago you didn't want to be alone."

"A couple hours ago I didn't realize I was losing my mind!"

He grabbed her wrist as she walked by. "Okay, okay. Calm down, Amara. Yelling isn't going to solve anything. If you just relax, we will get you through this."

"And what will happen when I do?"

"This is hard enough on your body as it is. If you don't calm down it's going to be worse."

That stopped her tirade. "Is it going to hurt?"

"Have you hurt so far?"

Not *hurt* exactly, just more of an uncomfortable sensation. "Well, not yet. But will it hurt later?"

"What do you mean?"

Oh, for God's sake. "When the, you know, change starts to happen."

He laughed. "It's already happened."

"But you said it could take weeks."

"It's been about that, hasn't it?"

She blinked. "Yes, I suppose it has."

She didn't like the way he hesitated. Taking a deep breath, she pulled her wrist out of his grasp. "What do *you* want from *me*?"

He looked at her like she was just as crazy as him. "Everything."

"*Everything?*" Well, wasn't that quite the answer? "I can't do this."

"It's kind of too late for that."

"It was an accident."

He shrugged. "Regardless, you can't take it back."

"There's nothing I can do?"

"You could try accepting it." He was beyond irritated now. "Accepting *me*."

Typical male. Here she was worrying about a major life change and he was taking it personally. "Cut the crap. I *do* accept you, and you know that."

"As what?"

As a total nut job who thinks—who *is* a vampire.

If she accepted Marco for what he really was, she would have to accept what she was, too. She was *so* not ready for that. It was bad enough when she started to notice a couple of gray hairs. This was too much to take.

But if she didn't accept him, he'd be crushed. She had a hard time picturing the big guy crushed, but he would be. He wouldn't show it, that wouldn't be the macho thing to do, but he'd be devastated.

So, what was she supposed to do?

"Hey, Mr. Scary. At least you could have warned me about what would happen if I, you know, *drew a little blood*."

He laughed. "Is that a common occurrence for you?"

"Drawing blood? I've been known to, on occasion."

His eyes widened in surprise. "Really? I hope you plan to do it again."

"That depends."

"On what?"

"If I ever decide to let you into my bed again."

The corner of his mouth lifted a little. "You don't have a choice."

"Ha! I choose how I live my life. Or unlife. Or whatever I'm supposed to call this."

"You're wrong on both counts, sweetheart." He got up from the chair and walked toward her, backing her against the wall. "Vampires are not undead. We're living and breathing, similar to humans. We just have much longer life spans and a different genetic code."

"Oh, yeah? What else was I wrong on?"

"You don't get to choose whether you have me or not. You're my woman, plain and simple."

"*Excuse me?* Where do you get off telling me something like that? I can make my own choices, thank you very much." Marco brushed his fingers over her breasts, barely concealed by the worn tee shirt she'd pulled on before coming downstairs. She blinked as his thumbs skimmed her nipples. She wanted so much to be angry at him for his comments, but she couldn't muster up enough of the emotion. He was baiting her again, toying with her because he knew it would make her angry. "Stop that!"

"Why? Don't you like it?"

"Whether or not I like it is beside the point. I'm trying to get it through your thick skull that I don't want you—"

He slipped his hand under the hem of her shirt and cupped her mound. "Funny, you feel like you want me."

"You didn't let me finish what I was saying. I don't want you referring to me as your woman. I'm my own person. I don't need you telling me what I can and cannot do."

"I don't plan on doing that. I just want you clear on the fact that this is a monogamous relationship. I don't want you running around with other men, and I won't touch another woman."

"Ever?"

"Ever."

She'd heard that before, but somehow she knew this time it was the truth. Monogamous? She could handle that, as long as they were both clear on the rules. He slid a finger into her already wet cunt and she lost her train of thought altogether. She tried for a token protest, but it came out sounding suspiciously like a moan. She was glad she hadn't bothered to put on panties this morning.

"Yeah, that's what I want." He leaned in closer and nipped her earlobe. His voice was a hot whisper against her sensitized skin. "You're so hot, so wet. I love how tight you are. You fit my cock so snugly, like a warm, wet glove. You were made for me, sweetheart. *Me*, and nobody else. No other man is ever going to touch you like this. Do you understand?"

She whimpered in agreement. She'd agree to dye her hair green and tattoo a dragon on her forehead if he'd just move his fingers a little to the left…

He continued. "I'm going to make you come, right here against the wall. Then I'm going to take you to bed and spend the rest of the day fucking you. We should both be sleeping, but I can't sleep at all when I'm around you. So we'll spend the day exploring each other's bodies instead. Do you want that?"

She nodded.

To her dismay, he stopped moving his hand. "Do you want me to fuck you, Amara?"

"Yes."

"What?"

"*I said yes*!" She cried out in frustration when he still held back.

"Yes, what?"

She didn't know what kind of games he was playing, but she didn't like them very much. She tried to shove him away, but it was like trying to move the Great Wall of China.

He bit into her neck enough for her to feel the sting. "Tell me what you want."

"I want you to go away!" She took a breath. "I want you to fuck me!"

"Yeah, I thought so."

He stroked his finger in and out of her. She wasn't about to let him torture her physically, not after what he'd just put her through mentally. She dragged her nails over his back, pressing hard enough that he could feel the scratch through his tee shirt. He moaned and pressed her harder against the wall, his breath escaping in a hiss. She smiled in satisfaction.

Her satisfaction was short lived. Marco turned the tables on her easily, spreading her legs wide and rubbing his thumb across her clit. When she was on the verge of orgasm, he pulled back.

She cried out, trying in vain to impale herself on him. It was no use, their position was too awkward.

"Knock it off, Marco."

He laughed. She wanted to punch him in the gut. Hard. Here she was, in absolute agony, and he was making a joke.

"Tell me what you want."

He was starting to lose his patience. She may not have known him long, but she'd known him long enough to know when he was about to crack. Poor baby. "I already told you."

She reached between them and unzipped his pants, pushing them and his boxers down his hips. Her knuckles brushed his cock on the way down and he groaned. Grabbing her legs, he wrapped them around his waist.

"I need to know you're mine. Forever." He slid his cock inside her once before he pulled out completely. "I need to hear you say it."

"Are you suddenly having a self-confidence problem?"

"Say it, Amara."

If she kept silent, she'd be left hot and bothered for the rest of the day. If she stopped torturing him and told him what he wanted to hear, which was what she wanted as well, they'd both be happy. "I'm yours. Forever. But you're mine, too. This has to be equal."

Chapter Sixteen

"I wouldn't have it any other way." He slammed his cock home, filling her cunt to the hilt. It just didn't get any better than this.

"Forever, Amara," he repeated. He didn't need to. She knew it as well as he did. She could protest all she wanted, but it all came down to the fact that she didn't want to be away from him again. The first time had been bad enough. She didn't even want to think about the next time.

His strokes were wild and erratic, pushing her to the edge quickly. Was there ever anything slow and easy with him? Not that she was complaining—her sex life had never been so full. But she didn't think the man was capable of anything other than ravishment when it came to sex.

He was entirely too strong. It amazed her that he could hold her up for this long and not collapse under the pressure.

His lips grazed her cheekbones, her hairline, and her jaw line while he continued to drive her to the point of complete and total ecstasy. Derek, and all her other lovers for that matter, could take a lesson or two from Marco on how to make sure a woman was satisfied. She'd never had it this good. Why would she give it up, just because of the silly little fact that her lover was a vampire?

Wait a second—so was *she*.

She groaned at the thought. That was going to take a long time to get used to.

He nuzzled her neck. "You should feed again."

She couldn't argue with that, not when she was starting to crave the stuff like it was air. She sunk her teeth into his neck and drank briefly, but had to let him go when she came. She couldn't manage bucking, convulsing, and sucking at the same time.

Marco's release was right on the heels of her own. He spurted inside her, groaning against her neck. When she finally floated back to the real world, he set her down on her feet and kissed the top of her head.

"Is it really going to be that bad, being stuck with me for the rest of your life?"

She laughed against his chest. "That depends. How long is my life going to be?"

"Your natural life will be thousands of years."

She pursed her lips and rolled her eyes toward the ceiling, pretending to think it over.

"Amara." The tone in his voice was warning.

She sighed. "Well, I guess I can learn to live with it. Provided I don't have to run around biting strangers' necks for kicks."

"You won't ever have to feed off of anyone but me. I'll take care of you, and do the biting strangers' necks for both of us."

Finally, something besides sex to look forward to.

* * * * *

Amara woke up sometime later to the sound of voices. Male voices, and more than one. Was Royce around again?

She hoped not. She didn't need to deal with any more of his arrogant attitude. She sat up in bed and rubbed her face, wondering how she'd gotten upstairs. The last thing she remembered was collapsing in Marco's arms after the interlude in the kitchen.

Damn. Even when she'd lived with Derek, she'd never had sex so many times in one day. No wonder she was so tired lately.

She dressed quickly and wandered down the stairs, as quietly as she could, to try to hear a little of what they were saying. She jumped when she rounded the corner and literally bumped right into Marco.

"Yikes!"

He looked amused, but a little worried as well. "That'll teach you to sneak up on people."

She laughed nervously, trying to shrug it all off. "What are you two doing down here? You were so loud it sounded like you were having a party at the foot of the bed."

"Ha." Marco ran a hand through his hair. "We weren't that loud."

"Wanna bet?"

She went into the kitchen and poured herself a cup of coffee. In the end she dumped half the cup out, filling the mug to the brim with milk.

"Too strong?"

She nodded at Marco. "Everything seems to be like that lately. That's why I haven't been able to eat anything."

"Is she feeding?" That came from Royce, who had just stepped into the room. His long, sandy blond hair was flowing around his shoulders this time, and his bright floral patterned shirt and khaki pants had been replaced by a plain black tee shirt and well-worn jeans. He looked different, better. He looked…like Marco with lighter hair.

Just what she needed—not one, but two hulky, sulky vampires hounding her every move and reminding her to eat every five seconds.

Amara rolled her eyes. "What do you care?"

He raised an eyebrow at her and for a second she saw him for the scholar Marco claimed he was. Then the easy-going, carefree mask slipped back into place and she was left wondering if she'd just witnessed some kind of illusion.

"I care a great deal. I don't want to see you kill yourself over this."

Oh, *okay*. First she was turning into a vampire and now she was suicidal? *Not likely*. "Listen, bud. I don't care who you are to Marco, or who you are at all. When I'm hungry, I will eat. Not before then, no sooner, so just get over it already."

Royce turned to Marco. "Is she always this difficult?"

Marco nodded.

"Has she fed yet?"

She put her hands on her hips. "Excuse me, but isn't that what got me into this mess in the first place?"

Marco closed his eyes and took a deep, slow breath. When he opened his eyes, barely contained anger was visible. "Yes, Amara, and yes, Royce. Now why don't the two of you try to get along?"

Yeah, and maybe a monkey would be the next president, she thought.

Royce frowned at her and she realized she must have spoken the thought out loud. She would have blushed, if she'd cared in the least what the jerk thought of her.

"Are you sure you want this one?" he asked Marco.

Marco nodded.

"There are so many to choose from. I could help you find a nice girl. One who isn't such a pain in the ass?"

Marco flashed her an evil smile. "No. She's perfect just the way she is."

She snorted.

Royce frowned again. "Oh, yeah. That's so painfully obvious."

She didn't like the sarcastic tone in his voice.

"Marco, what happened?" he continued. "You've gone nearly four hundred years without making this mistake. How could you let it happen again?"

A shard of pain flashed in Marco's eyes. "Amara isn't like Sarah, and what happened with Sarah was no accident. She asked for it. When are you going to believe that?"

"I'm sorry. I don't understand why she would have asked you to turn her when I should have been able to give her everything she needed." Royce shook his head. "It doesn't matter how it happened, or why. You still made a mistake."

She cleared her throat. "Who the hell is Sarah?"

"His wife." Marco gestured to Royce. "My…mate."

"Your *what?*" She fumed. "You had better start explaining yourself pretty quickly, bud, because you're about to get a dose of garlic in your eyes."

Royce laughed. "Garlic?"

Marco gave him a strange look. "You know, those stupid movies."

Was he ever going to get over it? "You mean those movies that made me practically a cult figure? The ones that also made me piles of money?" She didn't want to mention how that money had been spent.

Neither of them paid any attention to her until she clapped her hands together. "Hello? Is *anyone* listening?"

Royce sighed. "Unfortunately, we're not being given much of a choice."

She tried to sock him, but he dodged her fist easily. Now he looked like he was going to laugh, too.

"Well, boys, I'm glad you're having a good laugh at my expense. But I asked you a question and if I don't get my answer soon someone's going to be hurting."

It would probably be her, and all three of them knew it. She pressed on anyway. "So, Marco dear, did you forget to mention the fact that you already have a mate?"

He held his hand up. "Relax for minute and listen to me. You're too worked up. It isn't healthy."

"Do I look like I care what's healthy?" She was too pissed to stop now.

"Amara, please. Sarah's nothing. Just listen—"

She blinked. "Wait a second, this isn't some kind of personal harem deal, is it? Because I don't want any part of that. I'm open to new things, but I'm not interested in being one of a thousand women."

"No, no harems involved," he said. "There's only you. Sarah's dead."

Chapter Seventeen

Royce was kind enough to make himself scarce while Marco explained their unusual circumstances to Amara. That was a good thing. He didn't want Royce yelling about his mistakes while he tried to deal with Amara's tantrum.

He took her back into the living room and sat her down on the couch. She didn't give him a chance to speak.

"Why didn't you tell me you were married more than once?"

He sighed. "I'm not married now. There was only the one time, four hundred years ago. Sarah was Royce's wife, not mine."

"What the hell is going on here?" she demanded. He could see the anger in her eyes.

He had to give her credit though. She'd been through so much in the past couple of weeks. He was lucky she hadn't tried to murder him by now.

He took a deep breath and began. "From the minute I saw Sarah, I knew I had to have her. Nothing was going to stop me. I took advantage of her, and that was wrong. Of course, I was young and stupid then."

Amara snorted. "So what's changed?"

He laughed. "I'm not so young anymore. Anyway, there were only two problems when it came to Sarah. One, I'm not exactly human, and two, she was married to my brother."

He let that sink in for a minute.

She blinked. "Wait a second. Royce is your brother?"

He nodded.

"And you didn't bother to mention that sooner? You guys don't seem that close."

"Stealing your brother's wife tends to break up the relationship." He sighed. "We're working it out, but it's taken the better part of four hundred years."

"How long ago did this happen?"

"About five years after I turned."

Amara nodded, then shook her head. "Why would you do that to your brother?"

"I told you. I'd only been a vampire for five years, and I hadn't yet learned to control my urges. As you know firsthand, I still have a little trouble with that. When I saw her, I had to have her, so I did what I could to get her."

"And he just let you pursue his wife without stepping in? Did he give you permission?"

"He didn't even know I was alive." He laughed humorlessly at the memory. "I didn't want anyone to know what I'd become. It wasn't exactly accepted in those days."

"It's not very accepted now, either."

"Yeah, I can tell that from the popularity of your movies and hundreds of others. Anyway, Royce was a little pissed when he found out Sarah was leaving him. Also, he was upset with me for not coming to him when I was first turned. He was a healer back in those days, and he thought he might have been able to cure me. The problem was, I wasn't looking for a cure."

She nodded. "Go on."

"He didn't see what I had to offer her that he didn't. Now that I look back on it, I realize he was right." He ran a hand through his hair, distraught with the memories. "Sarah asked me to turn her, but she didn't handle the change well. She killed herself within the first year. So within six years, I'd lost two women close to me."

"You loved Sarah?"

He shook his head. "No. That's the worst part. I didn't love her at all. I wanted to possess her, but love didn't even enter the equation."

"Possess? Like you're doing with me?" Her voice was barely above a whisper.

"No. No man could ever possess you." He feathered a touch across her cheek. "What I feel for you is different than what I've felt for any other woman."

"Annoyance?"

He laughed. "No. Well, not always."

She sighed heavily, looking irritated and confused. "Then what is it you feel for me?"

Love. But he wasn't ready to confess that yet. "Protectiveness. After all, it's my fault you're in this situation."

"*Protectiveness?* Is that all?" She looked doubtful.

He shrugged, uncomfortable with the strength of his feelings for her.

"How could you feel protective of me? You kidnapped me, ruined my life, and scared me with all these stories of dead women. That's kind of far from protecting me, Marco."

"I scared you, and I'm sorry. But I just want to take care of you and see that you don't get hurt again."

"*Right.* Sure you do." She huffed for a few minutes, but then curiosity got the better of her. "So if Royce is your brother that makes him four hundred years old, too."

"Give or take a few years." He winked at her. "We age pretty well, huh?"

She rolled her eyes. "Did you turn him, too?"

"Uh, no." He laughed. "After what happened with his wife, he found someone else to turn him."

"Why?"

"I suspect either to torture me until the end of eternity, or in an attempt to get Sarah back. He was too late."

"Would you have let her go?"

He shrugged. "I already had."

"You left a new vampire to fend for herself? Why would you do something like that?" Her eyes widened, as if she'd just remembered something. "You told me you killed your wife."

"Did I?" He shook his head, amused with her assumption. "What I told you was that I was to be put to death for her murder. Not once did I confess to such a crime, then or now."

"You didn't do it?"

"Of course I didn't do it." Did she have so little faith in him? "I would never kill anyone other than in self-defense. Elizabeth was about as defenseless as you could get, despite her affairs."

She raised her eyebrows at him. "You didn't kill her lover, either?"

"Which one?"

"She had more than one?"

He nodded. "She had two that I know of. Unfortunately one turned out to be a demon. When she wouldn't leave me, or the other man, for him, Tomaz got a little angry."

"He killed her?"

Marco nodded. "Yeah. And I took the blame."

"A demon, huh?"

He could see the disbelief in her eyes, and it almost made him laugh. "You know, Amara, it wouldn't hurt for you to open your mind a little."

She rolled her eyes. "I'm working on it. Talk about a crash course in all things paranormal. What happened to Tomaz?"

He shrugged. "I have no idea. He just disappeared after Elizabeth's death."

"Oh."

He could see her mentally blocking out most of the story. He'd have to deal with it later. Right now they had a few things to take care of.

"Amara—"

He was interrupted by a knock on the door. In an impressive display of speed, Amara jumped up from the couch and rushed to the door. He was surprised she only knocked over one lamp on the way.

He heard her sharp intake of breath as she swung the door open. "Derek!"

Derek? Who the hell was Derek, and what did he want with *his* woman?

"Baby, I'm so sorry for what I put you through. You've got to take me back."

Okay, he was going to have to kick this guy's ass. Nobody tried to take his woman and lived.

He got up from the couch and walked to the door.

Amara turned to him. "Um, Marco, this is Derek."

"What the hell do you want?" He recognized Derek right away as Amara's costar in those hideous movies. This was her former fiancé. He wasn't going to stand for this shit.

Derek pushed his way inside. "I want my fiancée back."

Marco shook his head. "Not happening. You gave her up. She's mine now."

Derek turned to Amara. "You've got to be kidding me. It's only been a few months since we broke up."

"You call what happened a breakup?" Amara poked Derek's chest with her finger. "I kicked you out, slime-ball, *after* you berated me for not wanting my sex life filmed for all the world to see. To make things worse, I caught you on tape with a whole group of women, and live in our bedroom with the man next door in the same ten minutes. Do you really think I'm just going to jump right back into bed with you? Not in this lifetime, buddy."

"Think about it for a minute, Amara. We could make so much money together. You would never have to wish for anything again. We'd be set for life."

"The only thing I wish for right now is that your dick shrivels up and falls off and you can't fuck anyone ever again, on camera or off. Even *Robby*."

Derek's mouth opened and closed, but no words came out. It was then that Marco noticed Amara's fangs.

Shit. No wonder good old Derek looked ready to pee his pants. Marco grabbed Amara's arm and pulled her behind him. Then he punched Derek in the jaw and the man crumpled to the floor.

Chapter Eighteen

"What did you do?" Amara looked scandalized.

Marco shook his head. "Go get Royce. We've got to figure something out."

"You killed him! You told me you'd never kill anyone, and you just killed him for no reason."

"He's not dead. He's just unconscious." He ran a hand through his hair. "Go get Royce. Now. And pull your fangs back in just in case he wakes up."

"Fangs?" She brought her hand to her mouth, her fingers skimming along the sharp points of her teeth. Her eyes widened. "When did this happen?"

"When you were yelling at Derek. You should probably keep better control of your temper until you learn to control the teeth."

"I didn't even notice."

"I'm sure you didn't. That's the reason I don't want you left alone. Now for the last time, please go get Royce. I need his help."

She nodded and ran down the hall to the den, where Royce had gone to watch TV while she and Marco had talked. She came back a few minutes later with Royce in tow. He didn't look very happy to be disturbed from what Marco suspected had been a nap.

"What the hell did you do this time, Marco?"

Marco shot a glance to Amara. "She showed him her fangs. He got a little nervous."

"Don't you blame this one all on me. *You're* the one who punched him."

"Would you rather he ran around telling everyone you're a vampire? I'm sure there are quite a few scientists out there who would love to get a hold of you."

Amara pursed her lips, her hands on her hips. "Oh, please. This is L.A. *Everyone* here is nuts. There are even a couple of clubs downtown that cater to people who think they're vampires. They wouldn't have believed him."

She had a point there. Still, he wasn't going to take any chances with his life, or his woman's.

Amara raised an eyebrow at him. "I'm not a possession."

He blinked hard. "Excuse me?"

"You need to stop thinking about me as your woman. You don't own me, Marco."

That was really creepy. "Have you been able to do that all your life, or is this something new?"

"Do what?" She frowned. "I don't know what you're talking about."

"Read minds."

She shook her head and sighed, looking very annoyed. "I told you this already. I don't read minds. I just get feelings every once in a while. Just like everybody else."

"No, *not* like everybody else. Didn't you even once in your life think this was an unusual skill?"

Royce looked at them, obviously fascinated by the conversation. "She reads minds?"

Marco shrugged. "It would appear that she ca[illegible] grandmother was a psychic."

"Makes sense that she'd be more observant than the average vampire, then."

"Please. My grandmother was a fortune-teller in one of those chintzy shops that the tourists love back in Vermont. It's nothing."

Royce ignored her. "Let's get him on the couch before he wakes up." He turned to Amara. "Can you do mind control?"

"You're kidding, right? I can't even make up my *own* mind. How am I supposed to do it for someone else?"

Royce rolled his eyes. "Can you try?"

"Can't *you* do it?" she asked.

"Actually, no. It takes a very long time to develop those kinds of skills, unless you're born with them."

"Well, I most certainly wasn't born with anything like that."

Marco wondered if he was going to have to drag her through every part of her new life kicking and screaming. "Just give it a try, okay?"

She shrugged. "Whatever."

She settled down on the couch next to Derek, who was starting to moan and stir. Suddenly his eyes snapped open and he looked around, his gaze settling on Marco. "You punched me! I should sue you for that!" Then his gaze settled on Amara. "What the hell *are* you? Is this some kind of joke?"

She shrugged, looking bored. "I don't know what you're talking about."

"You had fangs!"

"You must have real life confused with the movies again, honey." She spoke to him like she was speaking to a toddler, slowly and carefully enunciating every syllable. "I have fangs when I'm in costume, because my *character* is a vampire. As a human, *in real life,* my teeth are perfectly normal. See?" She flashed him a wide smile.

Derek nodded, but didn't look quite convinced.

"Are you snorting coke again, honey?" She batted her eyelashes at him and he blinked. Marco was amazed at the display. She didn't need mind control. She had enough attitude to accomplish the task, and then some.

Derek started to shake his head, but then turned sheepish. "I'm sorry, baby. I know I promised to stop, and I did for a long time. But when you made me leave I couldn't help it. I needed something to take an edge off the pain of losing you."

"You know what, Derek? You're an idiot. I kicked you out, and it was the best move I ever made. You did me a big favor by being an unfaithful jerk with no morals. If you hadn't totally screwed up my life, I never would have met Marco, who makes me happier in bed than you could ever hope to."

Derek blinked and turned to Marco. "Are you sleeping with my fiancée?"

"She's not your fiancée anymore."

Derek lunged at Marco, but Amara's swift kick to his gut sent him tumbling to the ground, doubled over in pain. "Get out of my house, Derek, before I call the police and have you arrested for harassment."

"You can't do that. That's bullshit."

"Then I could always tell them about the cocaine you have in your pocket. I'm sure they'd love to bust you again for possession." She tapped her fingernails on the phone that sat on an end table. "How about it, *honey*?"

Derek's eyes filled with fright and he hustled out of there before Amara could issue another threat.

Royce laughed after Derek slammed the door behind him. "You really know how to hit him where it hurts."

She shrugged. "He's already been arrested too many times. One more time and he goes to jail."

Marco could just imagine what would happen to someone like Derek Sanders in jail. He had to admit, the idea held more than a little appeal.

"Don't even think about it." Amara glared at him.

He laughed. "I wouldn't dream of it, sweetheart."

*****

Marco woke up from his extended nap at a little after ten that night. He rolled his head from side to side and stretched, wondering why Amara wasn't in bed with him. He was going to have to get her on a better sleep schedule before he went insane from lack of sleep.

Smelling freshly brewed coffee, the one thing he could still tolerate in small doses, Marco wandered down to the kitchen. Amara was standing at the stove, cooking of all things. The smell of the meat frying in the pan hit him, making him lose his appetite.

"What are you doing?"

"Royce went out to get a bottle of wine. I thought I'd make something to go with it."

More than likely Royce went out to feed and didn't want to upset Amara with that knowledge. "Why bother cooking? You don't need to eat it."

She shrugged. "It's habit, okay? Give me a little while to accept this change."

He could understand how she was feeling. He'd been through it himself, so many years ago. "Okay. What are you making?"

"Chicken." She scooped the chicken from the pan and put it on a plate. Slicing off a small chunk, she blew on it before she popped it into her mouth. "Actually, this isn't bad."

"What did you put on it?"

"Nothing." She looked surprised. "I would have thought it would be boring."

"Your senses are too heightened to enjoy seasoned food. If you still feel the need to eat actual food, keep it simple and it won't taste so bad," he said. "Of course, you no longer need food to survive, as long as you feed on a regular basis."

She frowned, her expression doubtful. But then she smiled and ignored his comment. "Do you want some?"

He shook his head. "I prefer to keep my diet liquid."

She winked. "I wasn't talking about the chicken."

She set the plate on the counter and beckoned him to her. Forgetting that he was just about to sneak out to feed, he walked toward her and pulled her closer. "Yeah, I could go for a little bit of you right now."

Placing his hands on her hips, he drew her tightly against him before he kissed her. Amara moaned and melted against him. She was so damned responsive—he loved it. It thrilled him that he would have this, have *her*, for the rest of his life. And that was a very long time.

This was where he belonged. Kidnapping her had been a dumb idea, more than dumb, but Ellie was wrong about one thing. Something good *had* come of it—he'd found the woman he wanted to spend forever with.

He just hoped Amara felt the same.

Would she get sick of him in a hundred years? *Sooner*? Would she leave when she learned to take care of herself and didn't need him anymore? He hoped not. He didn't want to live without her. He'd already lost two women, and they hadn't meant to him what Amara did. If she left, he wouldn't want to live anymore.

Whoa. Wait a second, when did he become such a fatalist?

Amara pulled away and glared at him. "Where are you?"

"I'm right here." He tried to kiss her again, but she stopped him with a hand over his mouth.

"No, you're not. Your body is here, but your mind is somewhere else. If you aren't going to focus on me, then maybe we should just forget this whole thing."

He shook his head. "I am focusing on you, but you're distracting me."

"How so?"

"Every time I try to think about being with you now, I get worried about you leaving in the future."

She hit him playfully on the shoulder. "I'm not going anywhere, you big idiot."

"You're not?" He shook his head. "I thought you didn't want this life."

She rolled her eyes. "I don't exactly have a choice, do I? Besides, I'd already decided I wanted to stay with you before I found out you turned me into a blood-drinking freak."

"You've mentioned that. I still don't understand why."

"Well, duh. I love you. I swear men can be such morons sometimes."

"You love me?"

"Yeah. Funny, huh? I hardly know you. I don't get along with your family. You don't like my cooking, but I can't seem to get enough of you. Strange how life works sometimes."

"Yeah, strange."

She loved him. He knew he was smiling like an idiot, but he couldn't help it. He'd gone so many years without love, and he was going to let himself enjoy this now.

"Okay, I suppose you're not going to say anything?"

He winked at her and pressed his body against her. "What do you want me to say?" He leaned in and nipped her neck. She moaned, but she tried to push him away.

"You're the one who was getting all mushy with the 'future without me' stuff. Now you're just going to ignore me?"

"Does it feel like I'm ignoring you?" He thrust his pelvis against hers, making sure she felt how hard he was. "Believe me, sweetheart, I'm not planning on ignoring you. In fact, I plan on doing just the opposite."

He cupped her breasts, barely covered in the thin robe she wore, and brushed his thumbs over her nipples. They instantly pebbled. He hoped she'd continue to walk around the house practically naked, even after they'd been together for a few thousand years.

His cock strained against the confines of his
thrust against her again, enjoying the sweet agony of be
so close, but not quite touching. He knew she wasn't done berating him yet, but when her tantrum was over, he planned to take her back to bed. First for a lot of sex, then for a little sleep.

Amara cleared her throat. "So you're going to pretend I didn't just tell you I love you?"

He laughed. Why was it that he couldn't resist teasing her? He licked her jaw. "Love? Is that what this discussion is about?"

He parted her robe and ran his hands along her hot skin. His whole body quivered and he nearly lost it right there when she unzipped his pants and slipped her fingers inside. She ran her hand along his cock and he shivered, almost forgetting what he needed to say.

"Yes, love." She ran the pads of her fingers over the head of his cock. He nearly jumped out of his skin. He grabbed her wrist, but she shook him off. "If you want this to go any further, you'd better start talking right now, buddy."

"Yeah, I suppose I love you."

She snorted. "Suppose?"

She tortured him with her fingers for barely five seconds until he gave in. "Okay, fine. I love you. I've loved you since you slammed me in the face with the teakettle. I will always love you. Just don't ever forget that, okay?"

"Why would I forget?" The confused look on her face was sweet.

"You might get sick of me after a while. Do you think you can wake up next to me every day and not eventually want to go out and find someone new?" He kept his tone light, but he was genuinely worried about that. It had happened once, and the marriage hadn't been hundreds of years old when it did.

"I could say the same thing about you. You've traveled the world, and seen so much. You've lived so long. How could you ever be content with me?" She bit her lip. "Am I going to be enough to keep you happy?"

"There aren't any guarantees in life, but the one thing I can promise you is that I'll love you for the rest of my life." He shrugged. "Whether that's a few years or a thousand, who's to say? But I'll give you everything I have for as long as I'm around."

Marco heard the doorknob turn and decided it was time to take this upstairs. He started to lead Amara out of the kitchen, but she stopped him. "What about Royce? He went to get—"

"I think he'll understand." Without waiting for her to protest further, he lifted her into his arms and carried her up the stairs to her bedroom.

Or was it their bedroom? There was still so much they needed to discuss. "Have you given any thought to where you want to live?"

"What's wrong with right here?" She unbuttoned his shirt and pushed it off his shoulders. He let it drop to the floor. Her robe came off next, followed by the rest of his clothes.

"It's kind of noisy. I'm not really into living in the city."

"It's not like we're in the center of downtown. This is a nice place to live."

"Too many neighbors. I like my privacy." He bent to run his tongue over one of her hardened nipples. She shivered.

"Where would you rather live?"

He paused. "I was thinking my place would be better."

"Way out there in the middle of the woods?"

"Yeah. It's quiet." Quiet was a good thing. "There are no nosy neighbors and annoying ex-fiancés."

He plunged his fingers deep inside her cunt, hoping to convince her one way or the other that his place would be a much better choice. She rocked her hips and whimpered.

When she spoke her voice was no more than a whisper. "As much as I'm enjoying this discussion, could we save it for another time? I'd rather concentrate on getting you into bed, and deal with where we're going to live later."

"But you are going to live with me, right?"

"Yes." Her answer was more of a hiss as he flicked her clit with his thumb. "Now shut up and make love to me, will you?"

He wouldn't turn down that kind of demand. Ever. He lowered her to the bed and covered her body with his. He looked deep into her eyes. She was so beautiful, and he didn't know what he'd done to deserve her. But he wasn't going to question it, and he wasn't going to walk away from her. She was his, damn it, and he wasn't ever going to let her go.

He stroked her hair as he kissed her deeply, trying to show her just how much he loved her. He'd never be able to express fully, in words, the depths of his feelings for her. He just didn't have it in him to be that poetic. He'd have to show her in other ways how much she meant to him.

Maybe he'd even get to like those stupid movies, if that's what it took. He had to admit, she looked hot in black vinyl.

Amara bit his ear. "You're far away again."

"Sorry."

"I can't let you do that. I need you right here with me."

He nodded and kissed her again. Her lips parted and he drove his tongue into her mouth. She reciprocated, sucking on his tongue. It was incredible. *She* was incredible.

Without warning, Amara flipped him over onto his back. She straddled him and impaled herself on his throbbing cock. She started to move, but he held her still with his hands on her hips, intent on savoring the feeling of being this connected with her. When he was with her, it felt like they were one.

He'd never felt a connection like this with a woman before, vampire or not. Maybe it had something to do with her psychic heritage.

Obviously tired of waiting, Amara pushed his hands away and lifted herself until only the head of his cock was inside her. He groaned as she slid back down, all the way to the base. God, she felt so good. He bit her shoulder, savoring the taste of her.

He reached between them and stroked her clit. She sighed and moved faster, taking them both on an amazing ride. She came in minutes, bucking and screaming, and sent him into his own shattering release.

After, he held her tightly, not wanting to let her go.

"Hey." She stroked his hair, his bare chest, and his stubble-lined jaw. "You feel better now?"

He laughed. "Oh, yeah. I don't think I can feel any better than this."

"We'll see about that." She laughed with him. "I've decided where I want to live."

Epilogue

"I still think you're an idiot."

Marco gave Ellie a dirty look. "That seems to be a common opinion around here."

He looked at Amara for help, but she just shrugged. "What can I say? I have to agree with Ellie on this one."

"Kidnapping women is not the way to meet a mate, even if it does end well."

He rolled his eyes. Why he'd ever encouraged Amara to spend time with Ellie was beyond him. Now instead of having one woman on his case, he had five. Between Amara, Ellie, and Ellie's gaggle of female relatives, he couldn't get a break.

"That's enough ganging up on me, ladies. I bet you both have better things to do with your time."

Ellie shrugged. "Not really. In case you hadn't noticed, I don't have much of a life."

Maybe he'd have to find a way to fix that. Ellie was spending far too much time at their house instead of at home with her own family. He might even have a good solution. It was definitely something to think about.

He laughed to himself. For a guy who'd sworn never to commit again, he sure had done a complete change. Not only did he have a mate, a *wife*, no less, since Amara had insisted on a real, *private* wedding, but they'd just spent a hefty chunk of change buying and renovating an old mansion on the New England coast, in the small town where he'd first met Ellie and her family.

He and Royce had just about mended their tentative relationship, and Amara had left Hollywood and stupid movies behind for good.

"Okay, Mr. Introspective," Amara got his attention. "I have a proposition for you."

He raised an eyebrow. "Oh, yeah?"

"I've been thinking a lot about L.A. and my old job."

He nodded, not sure he liked where this was going. "Do you miss it?"

"Well, I don't really miss the city. But I do miss the job. I really liked horror movies."

He groaned. "Please don't tell me you're thinking of going back."

"*Please*. The commute alone would kill me." She got a wicked gleam in her eyes. "I'm thinking about writing a book instead."

He sighed. "Not a campy vampire story, I hope."

"Actually, that's exactly what I wanted to do." She laughed. "I think I'd be really good at it. After all, I have a little experience."

Ellie perked up. "That sounds great. I loved those Midnight movies."

Marco groaned. "God, Ellie. Whatever you do, don't encourage her."

"Don't start." Amara playfully swatted his arm. "I don't know what it is you have against making fun of yourself every once in a while. It wouldn't hurt to relax a little."

"I'll relax when you give up this stupid idea," he grumbled.

"Get used to it. Besides, writing would give me something to do when I stay home with the children."

He opened his mouth, but it was nearly a full minute before he could get any sound to come out. "Are you trying to tell me something?"

Amara laughed. "No, I'm not pregnant yet. But the look of sheer terror on your face is priceless."

He let out a breath and wiped his brow. That was a close one. He was just getting used to the idea of being married. He wasn't nearly ready to start thinking about children. "Maybe in a few hundred years we could try to have a family."

She shook her head, her expression devilish. "Are you kidding? I don't want to wait a couple hundred years. I want a family before I'm forty."

It was a good thing he loved Amara, because this was going to be a long life.

Enjoy this excerpt from

Dark Promises: Demonic Obsession

Chapter 1

Ellie sat on an old wooden bench, her sketch pad resting on her lap. The sunset just visible over the tops of the trees washed the sky in brilliant hues of orange and pink. The rustling of the summer wind through the leaves and the faint breaking of waves against the nearby shore calmed her nerves like nothing else could—on most nights.

Just not tonight.

She tucked a few stray strands of hair behind her ears and took a sip from her water bottle, making an attempt to ignore the strange sensations that prickled the hair on the back of her neck. The air crackled with an electrical tension, sending a shiver through her despite the warm temperature.

Something was different.

Something had disturbed the peaceful, sleepy quiet of Stone Harbor. Something she couldn't define—maybe didn't want to. A knot of anxiety formed in the pit of her stomach and her gaze landed on a man leaning against a tree a few dozen feet away. Did he have something to do with the disturbance?

"Yeah, right," she muttered to herself, turning her attention back to her sketch pad. He looked about average height, with an average build and average dark hair—nothing spectacular about him, at least from this distance. He wore khaki pants and an off-white polo shirt—nothing impressive there. He looked more like the married with three children type than the bad to the bone and out to cause trouble type.

So why couldn't she shake the feeling that his presence signaled danger?

She blew out a breath, frustrated with her paranoia. So her ex-husband had turned out to be a first-class jerk disguised as a successful businessman. That didn't mean that every other man who dressed nicely meant her emotional harm. If she didn't get over what happened with Todd, she'd never get the chance to meet a nice guy and settle down. Three years had passed since her divorce—plenty of time to get over her silly insecurities.

She had to stop pasting Todd's face on every man who walked into her life. They weren't *all* like him—she wasn't naïve enough to believe that—but her luck with men seemed to really suck lately. This poor guy hadn't done anything to her, he probably hadn't even noticed she was alive, and she'd already pegged him as some kind of deranged mass murderer.

His head was turned toward the small pond in the center of the park, but every so often, he looked in her direction. From the distance, she couldn't be sure if he was looking at *her*, but the fact that he might be unsettled her. Her fingers smoothed over the totem that hung from a silver chain around her neck—a small panther carved in black onyx—in a reaction that was more automatic than calculated. She closed her eyes briefly, calling to the animal the totem represented for guidance. She tried to focus on the sleek grace of the creature, the control and strength it exuded, but her powers of concentration were severely lacking tonight. It was all *his* fault.

She tried to keep her eyes off him, but she couldn't help stealing little glances every so often. Something about him compelled her to, even when she knew it was impolite and possibly dangerous. The man was a complete stranger in a town where she recognized most people on sight, and that fact alone made her wary. She knew she shouldn't stare, yet she couldn't pull her gaze away.

That frightened her the most. An odd fixation on a complete stranger was something she thought she'd outgrown years ago, once she'd hit puberty. What made him so special that she couldn't draw her gaze away, even with exercised concentration? As far as she could tell—*nothing*.

But there had to be *something*, or else she wouldn't be spending her evening observing him when she'd come here to sketch the sunset in preparation for her next painting.

His head swung in her direction and she didn't have time to look away. This time she had no doubts—he was looking right at her. She drew in a deep, shaky breath, her palms suddenly growing damp. A smile spread across his face and he nodded slightly—just enough to let her know he'd caught her staring. The thought unnerved her, but not enough to make her drag her gaze from his. A dog barking in the background finally broke the spell. She looked quickly back at her sketch pad, not wanting to encourage him in any way, but afraid it might already be too late.

She tried to make a rough sketch of the flowers lining the banks of the pond, but her traitorous hands instead drew the shadowy form of a lean, dark-haired man. After three attempts, she slammed her pencil down on the pad and sighed in disgust. It figured. She'd never felt a pull this strong—not even when she'd been with Todd. She prided herself on being independent, level-headed to a fault, and suddenly she felt like the world had tilted on its axis.

She was being such an idiot! Ellie was the calm one. Her sister, Charlotte, was the dramatic one. Always had been. But now it seemed like Ellie had switched places with her younger sister. The whole situation made her feel off balance, like she couldn't quite get her footing right. This had to be some kind of a sign that she needed to make some changes in her life. Either that, or she needed some kind of psychological counseling. She blew out a breath and muttered to herself, "Normal, healthy women don't obsess about complete strangers."

And all the while, the stranger in question was probably leaning against that tree, laughing to himself about the skinny girl who kept staring at him. He'd probably go home later to his house with a white picket fence and a couple of Volvos in the driveway and have a good laugh with his equally yuppyish wife.

Yeah, she was definitely nuts. Time to get back to work. That was, after all, her purpose for being in the park.

She tried her best to focus on her sketching, but it was no use. Her mind was on that man, not on her work. She slammed her pencil down on the pad yet again, this time with a lot more force. If she wasn't going to get anything done tonight, she might as well just pack up and go home. No sense wasting time sitting around gaping at strangers when she could be home in her studio—alone—getting some actual work done.

"Why did you stop?"

She nearly jumped a mile at the voice behind her. She spun around so quickly the pad and pencil slid out of her lap and hit the grass below.

It was *him*.

She opened her mouth to chastise him for sneaking up on her, but she couldn't form a single coherent sentence. Up close, he was even more fascinating then he'd been at a distance—and he certainly wasn't as *average* as she'd first thought. His hair was thick and shiny—a rich, deep brown nearly as dark as hers. The light colored shirt contrasted sharply with the golden bronze tone of his skin.

A half-smile played on his full lips, and she caught a glimpse of gleaming white teeth. "Are you an artist by trade?" he continued, his gaze snagging hers and holding tight. She couldn't look away, even if she'd wanted to. His eyes were a clear emerald green with small flecks of gold threaded through, almost hypnotic in their beauty. She'd never seen eyes that color in her life.

He cleared his throat and she realized she'd been staring. "You do speak English, don't you?" he asked, his tone laced with humor.

"What? Oh, English. Yeah." She cursed herself for sounding like a complete airhead, but she couldn't help it. They just didn't make them like this in Stone Harbor, and seeing him must have short circuited something vital in her brain.

"I asked if you were an artist."

She could do this. He was just a man. Nothing to be afraid of.

"Yes." She paused and took a deep breath. At least she'd been able to make some sense this time. A little calmer, she launched into an explanation. "A painter, but I work with charcoal from time to time when I need a change, which now I—."

She clamped her mouth shut and let a breath out through her nose. *Geez, Ellie. Think you can give him any* more *information he didn't ask for?* She mentally berated herself for nearly boring him to death. What would he care about her humdrum life? The only interesting things about her were things she only told her closest friends. The rest of her life—the public part—wasn't even worthy of a mention. Bending down, she scooped the pad and pencil off the ground and settled them back in her lap, covering the picture with her arms to block it from his view.

She lifted her gaze to him again, ready to excuse herself and make a quick exit before she humiliated herself further. He focused his eyes on her lap, presumably trying to get a glimpse of what she'd been drawing. It gave her a chance to get a better look at near-perfection. His face reminded her of a sculpture—all smooth lines and clean angles. She placed him somewhere in his late thirties or early forties, from the faint lines around his eyes and mouth. His hair, though, was dark without a hint of gray. And all that bronze skin looked unusually soft, and had the strange desire to run her fingertips over his cheeks to find out.

What a painting he'd make. She'd never ask a complete stranger to pose, but the thought intrigued her. A face like that would keep her hands—and eyes—busy for hours. The fading sun glinted in his eyes, and for a second they flashed gold. The sight made a shiver run down her spine, both from anxiety and something she hated to label as arousal.

"Who are you?" she asked when she finally got her mouth working properly. She supposed, if he planned to stand there and let her gape at him all night, he at least owed her an introduction. And if she knew his name, he wouldn't be a *complete* stranger anymore—and she wouldn't feel so guilty about staring.

"Eric Malcolm." He held out his hand and she took it hesitantly, expecting a handshake. When he brought her hand to his lips and brushed a kiss over her knuckles, she blinked in surprise. His palm was warm and soft, and the fleeting touch of his lips against her skin had her drawing a sharp breath.

"And you are…?" he continued, her hand still firmly in his grip.

Think. She mentally knocked herself on the head, trying to get her brain to function. "Ann Elizabeth Holmes."

Stupid! No one called her Ann Elizabeth. What was she thinking?

"Well, Ann Elizabeth—"

"Ellie." She smiled weakly. "Please. Call me Ellie. I hate Ann Elizabeth."

"Why?" He raised an eyebrow at her as he spoke.

"It's boring." *Oh, yeah. Like Ellie is any better.*

He frowned and studied her for a minute. "You don't strike me as a boring woman."

She had to laugh at that. "Stick around. I'll prove you wrong in a matter of days. Maybe even hours."

He nodded slowly, his eyes darkening almost imperceptibly. "I might just do that."

"Oh, no, I didn't mean…" She sighed, not willing to finish the thought. She felt a little like a moth drawn to flame. His gaze sucked her in, entranced her, but if she got close enough she'd be fried to a crisp. He could do that to her—she had no doubts about it.

"I think you did." He glanced at the pad in her lap, his head cocked to the side. Self-consciously she brushed her hair back behind her ears. He took full advantage of the moment, reaching over her shoulder and lifting the pad off her lap before she even had time to react.

"Hey! Give that back!" She made a grab for her sketch pad, but he held tight with one hand as he leafed through a couple of the pages with the other. He had to have noticed the sketches of him, but he didn't show any kind of a reaction.

"Why are you trying to hide this from me? Surely a woman as talented as you is used to showing off her work?"

The subject matter, rather than the work as whole, caused her the most distress. She didn't need him thinking she was some kind of obsessed mental case—*normal women didn't go around drawing pictures of complete strangers*. Yeah. If she kept repeating that, she might actually start to believe it.

She shrugged, failing miserably at casual. "I have a few in a gallery downtown. This," She yanked the pad out of his hands and closed the cover. "Is too raw to share. I make it a policy never to let anyone see my work when it's in the beginning stages." Especially if the work was of a man who had no idea she'd used him as an artist's model.

"That's too bad. It seems like such a waste to *not* share."

His compliment caught her off guard. She didn't know how to answer. "I guess I have doubts about that. Most artists do."

"Don't doubt your talent. If you consider these sketches rough, I'd be very interested in taking a look at some of your finished work."

"Why?" she asked, incredulous. Suspicion rose in her. That was taking the whole flattery thing a little too far.

"I'm redecorating my house, and I'm very interested in New England artists." He put his hands in his pockets and leaned a hip against the back of the bench. Everything about his manner said "casual", yet she detected a faint...restlessness about him that practically screamed "ulterior motives".

"Is that why you're in town? To acquire *art*?" She resisted the urge to tell him that the words "woman" and "stupid" were not synonymous. When people wanted art, they went to the big galleries in New York City. They didn't come to Stone Harbor. Sure, there were a couple of galleries downtown, but they were mostly for the tourists who flocked to the town in late summer to invade the beaches.

He elegantly shrugged one shoulder, the casual façade firmly in place. "Art is one of the reasons for my visit."

Business, perhaps? He didn't strike her as someone who traveled to the edge of nowhere for fun. She waited for him to elaborate on his other reasons, but he didn't. He just stood over her, his gaze boring into hers, until she couldn't take the silence anymore. "The gallery at the Art Association downtown has a few of my paintings. You could always go down there if you wanted to take a look. It's a little red brick building on the corner of Main and Washington. You can't miss it."

"I don't get a personal tour?" He smiled down at her and something quivered low in her stomach.

She almost gave in then and there. *Almost.* But then she remembered that, even in a tiny town like Stone Harbor, getting too friendly too quickly with strangers was a bad idea. "No, I don't think so. You look like a smart guy. I think you can find your way around a gallery all by yourself."

She had to get out of there—*now*, before she forgot all her common sense. She stood and left the bench, stuffed the pad and pencil into her tote bag, and started toward the parking lot without glancing back. If she looked, even a tiny bit, she knew part of her would want to stay. Funny, she'd always thought of herself as a rational woman. Talking to a complete stranger the way she did certainly wasn't rational. It bordered on insane.

"Would it change things if I told you I'm more interested in the artist than the art?"

She stopped in mid-stride and pivoted. "No. Definitely not. I—"The words she'd meant as forceful denial came out as no more than a squeak that ended in a gasp when she realized he stood less than two feet away.

"How did you get there?" He'd been all the way back by the bench, and she hadn't heard his footsteps behind her.

"The same as you. I walked." He shrugged and smiled, fixing that incredible green gaze on her and turning her body to jelly. She felt like he'd stepped even closer in the seconds that followed, but he hadn't moved at all.

"Sure you did." Yeah, and she was Mary, Queen of Scots. Thoughts in her head began sliding together like pieces in a puzzle, and she didn't think she'd like the final picture. "Listen, I really do have to go. I have things to do."

"That's too bad. It would be a shame to waste such a beautiful night. I'm sure, without all the lights of the big city, the night sky here is fabulous."

"It is. It's also dark. Very dark, and I have to get home before the sun sets." She had a feeling that she didn't want to be stuck alone with him after the sun went down. He made her nervous, suspicious—*tense*.

And aroused.

The last thought hit her like a slap in the face. The only thing she knew about him was name, and somehow he conjured such strong emotions within her that she couldn't control them.

"It will be a beautiful sunset, if you just stay a few more minutes," he continued with that deep, hypnotic voice.

She smiled nervously, shifting from foot to foot. The combination of unease and attraction was a powerful combination. "Yeah. It will. I hope you get a chance to enjoy it. If you'll excuse me…"

"Of course." He smiled ruefully. "If you insist on leaving, I won't stop you."

Then why did it feel like her legs were leaden, and she couldn't drag herself away without some serious effort?

"I—I have to go." She repeated the words like a mantra—one her body refused to acknowledge. Despite her best intentions, her feet remained planted to the ground as if she'd grown roots.

"You're unsure of me, aren't you?" He didn't look upset. Instead, his gaze held sparks of humor and curiosity—and a healthy dose of the crippling arousal currently assaulting her.

She nodded slowly, nervously wetting her lower lip with the tip of her tongue. She backed up a step, then another, to put some much needed distance between them.

"I wouldn't expect a beautiful woman like you to be all alone. Do you have a man waiting at home for you?" His eyes darkened at the question.

He didn't know the half of it. Sometimes she *wished* she were all alone. One day with her family, and he'd understand. She shook her head. "It's just…I…never mind." She should leave before this got any worse, but her stubborn feet refused to move.

He stepped closer and raised his hand, a set of keys dangling from his fingers. *Her* keys. Her heart stopped for a beat before starting again with a thud. "Where did you get those?"

"On the ground by the bench. They must have fallen out of your bag." He held them in front of him as if daring her to come and get them.

She swallowed hard. She always kept her keys in her pocket or purse. *Always.* She never put them in her bag. That thought was enough to release her from whatever held her to the spot. "Thanks for bringing them to me." She held out her hand and waited for him to place them in her palm.

He laughed softly as he walked to her. "Here you are. Have a safe drive home." His fingers brushed her palm as he gave her the keys. She felt the contact all the way to her toes. His voice was a husky whisper—one that had her thinking illicit thoughts about naked, sweaty bodies tangled in satin sheets, moving together in—

"Thanks," she said sharply, trying to pull herself out of her lust-induced haze. What was wrong with her? It was like some wanton flake had crawled into her mind and set up residence.

"My pleasure." He lowered his head a little, his gaze meeting hers dead-on. His deep voice had her practically panting at his feet. "I meant what I said about your talent—and your beauty."

The sincerity in his gaze made her face flame. "Well, thanks. I really do have to go now. Again."

"I'll be in town for a while, and I plan to take a trip to the gallery you mentioned to see your paintings," he said as she turned to walk away. "Maybe I'll see you later."

"Maybe," she said without turning back to him.

She virtually ran toward her car. He didn't follow, and she didn't care. The pull he had over her rattled her, and if she hadn't walked away that second there was no telling what stupid things she might have done. She shifted her tote bag on her shoulder and walked faster. When she glanced up after she opened her car door, he hadn't moved an inch. Funny, but it felt as if he were standing right next to her.

It took about five minutes for everything to click firmly into place. She'd known, subconsciously, almost from the beginning of their meeting, but she hadn't dared acknowledge it until now. The truth hit her all at once when she paused at a stop sign. She didn't know *who* the stranger in the park was, but she knew *what* he was.

A vampire.

Just what she needed in her life—another vampire. She leaned forward and banged her head on the steering wheel a few times. "*Wonderful.*" She had a serious case of lust, and the guy wasn't even *human*.

And she'd bet her entire year's salary that the real reason for his visit had nothing to do with art.

* * * * *

Eric sat at the tiny round table, the blue light from the screen of his laptop the only illumination in the hotel room. He shifted in his chair and glanced at the glowing green digits on the alarm clock. Twelve fifteen. The night had just begun. He rubbed a hand down his face and thought about the woman in the park. Ellie. She might prove to be a distraction, if he wasn't careful. He had a job to do, and he'd be wise not to forget it.

He'd shaken her. That much had been obvious—barely. She was strong. Getting close to her wouldn't be as easy as he'd previously thought. He'd tried his hardest to bend her mind to his will, but he'd scarcely been able to get inside. Every time he thought he had her, she mentally locked him out. Sam had told him the woman was an ordinary human. Obviously, that was not the whole truth. But he'd do what it took to bend her—out of necessity. She might be his last chance at catching a killer before he destroyed another life. He had a personal stake in this job—three of his closest friends were dead.

He might be next, if he wasn't careful.

He'd have to be. Tracking the killer while having to constantly look over his shoulder had become tedious work. It had been months, and it was time to end this for good—no matter what it took. But he didn't want Ellie hurt.

Where that thought came from, he had no idea. He'd need to remember that he was here in Stone Harbor to do a job, *not* pursue a woman—at least no more than the job entailed. If he could get close to her, he'd be able to get the information he needed. It was quite possible, given her friendships with the few vampires who lived in town, that she already knew the killer's identity. But those vamps were a secretive bunch, so she might not know anything at all. That was why he'd have to get close to the human woman, get her to relax around him enough that he could get inside her head.

And he was fooling himself if he thought that was his only reason for wanting to get close to her. The second she'd looked up at him with those big blue eyes, lust had hit him with the force of a hurricane. He *wanted* to get to know her better, both mentally and physically, in a way that had absolutely nothing to do with work. But getting closer to her might mean putting up with her vampire friends for a little while, too, and that thought turned his stomach. The last thing he needed were a bunch of vamps to ruin his life, especially those few in particular.

God, he hated bloodsuckers.

About the author:

Elisa Adams Born in Gloucester, Massachusetts, Elisa Adams has lived most of her life on the east coast. Formerly a nursing assistant and phlebotomist, writing has been a longtime hobby. Now a full time writer, she lives on the New Hampshire border with her husband and three children. Welcomes mail from readers. You can write to her c/o Ellora's Cave Publishing, Inc.® 1056 Home Avenue, Akron OH 44310-3502.

Why an electronic book?

We live in the Information Age—an exciting time in the history of human civilization in which technology rules supreme and continues to progress in leaps and bounds every minute of every hour of every day. For a multitude of reasons, more and more avid literary fans are opting to purchase e-books instead of paperbacks. The question to those not yet initiated to the world of electronic reading is simply: *why?*

1. *Price.* An electronic title at Ellora's Cave Publishing runs anywhere from 40-75% less than the cover price of the exact same title in paperback format. Why? Cold mathematics. It is less expensive to publish an e-book than it is to publish a paperback, so the savings are passed along to the consumer.
2. *Space.* Running out of room to house your paperback books? That is one worry you will never have with electronic novels. For a low one-time cost, you can purchase a handheld computer designed specifically for e-reading purposes. Many e-readers are larger than the average handheld, giving you plenty of screen room. Better yet, hundreds of titles can be stored within your new library—a single microchip. (Please note that Ellora's Cave does not endorse any specific brands. You can check our website at www.ellorascave.com for customer recommendations we make available to new consumers.)
3. *Mobility.* Because your new library now consists of only a microchip, your entire cache of books can be taken with you wherever you go.

4. *Personal preferences are accounted for.* Are the words you are currently reading too small? Too large? Too...ANNOYING? Paperback books cannot be modified according to personal preferences, but e-books can.
5. *Innovation.* The way you read a book is not the only advancement the Information Age has gifted the literary community with. There is also the factor of what you can read. Ellora's Cave Publishing will be introducing a new line of interactive titles that are available in e-book format only.
6. *Instant gratification.* Is it the middle of the night and all the bookstores are closed? Are you tired of waiting days—sometimes weeks—for online and offline bookstores to ship the novels you bought? Ellora's Cave Publishing sells instantaneous downloads 24 hours a day, 7 days a week, 365 days a year. Our e-book delivery system is 100% automated, meaning your order is filled as soon as you pay for it.

Those are a few of the top reasons why electronic novels are displacing paperbacks for many an avid reader. As always, Ellora's Cave Publishing welcomes your questions and comments. We invite you to email us at service@ellorascave.com or write to us directly at: 1056 Home Avenue, Akron OH 44310-3502.

The Ellora's Cave Library

Stay up to date with Ellora's Cave Titles in Print with our Quarterly Catalog.

Lady Jaided Regular Features

Jaid's Tirade

Jaid Black's erotic romance novels sell throughout the world, and her publishing company Ellora's Cave is one of the largest and most successful e-book publishers in the world. What is less well known about Jaid Black, a.k.a. Tina Engler is her long record as a political activist. Whether she's discussing sex or politics (or both), expect to see her get up on her soapbox and do what she does best: offend the greedy, the holier-than-thous, and the apathetic! Don't miss out on her monthly column.

Devilish Dot's G-Spot

Married to the same man for 20 years, Dorothy Araiza still basks in a sex life to be envied. What Dot loves just as much as achieving the Big O is helping other women realize their full sexual potential. Dot gives talks and advice on everything from which sex toys to buy (or not to buy) to which positions give you the best climax.

On the Road with Lady K

Publisher, author, world traveler and Lady of Barrow, Kathryn Falk shares insider information on the most romantic places in the world.

Kandidly Kay

This Lois Lane cum Dave Barry is a domestic goddess by day and a hard-hitting sexual deviancy reporter by night. Adored for her stunning wit and knack for delivering one-liners, this Rodney Dangerfield of reporting will leave no stone unturned in her search for the bizarre truth.

A Model World

CJ Hollenbach returns to his roots. The blond heartthrob from Ohio has twice been seen in Playgirl magazine and countless other publications. He has appeared on several national TV shows including The Jerry Springer Show (God help him!) and has been interviewed for Entertainment Tonight, CNN and The Today Show. He has been involved in the romance industry for the past 12 years, appearing on dozens of romance novel covers and calendars. CJ's specialty is personal interviews, in which people have a tendency to tell him everything.

Hot Mama Cooks

Sex is her food, and food is her sex. Hot Mama gives aphrodisiac a whole new meaning. Join her every month for her latest sensual adventure -- with bonus recipe!

Empress on the Mount

Brash, outrageous, and undeniably irreverent, this advice columnist from down under will either leave you in stitches or recovering from hang-jaw as you gawk at her answers to reader questions on relationships and life.

Erotic Fiction from Ellora's Cave

The debut issue will feature part one of "Ferocious," a three-part erotic serial written especially for Lady Jaided by the popular Sherri L. King.

ELLORA'S CAVE
ROMANTICA PUBLISHING

Printed in the United States
35500LVS00005B/1-66

9 781419 950490